A
HAUNTING
IN
OREGON

A HAUNTING IN OREGON

MICHAEL RICHAN

DANTULL

By the author

The Bank of the River
A Haunting in Oregon
Ghosts of Our Fathers

A HAUNTING IN OREGON

ISBN-10: 1-49091-858-2 / ISBN-13: 978-1-49091-858-7

Published by Dantull (1480253)

First printing: September 2013

www.michaelrichan.com

For Kym

One

It looks haunted.

Their car emerged from the long, forested driveway and into the clearing where Mason Manor rose from the forest floor. It gave the impression of a fortress.

Steven had looked at pictures on the internet, but they didn't do it justice. Whoever designed it had drama in mind, a desire to make a statement. It had a central building of dark wood and brick walls, and extensions sprawled outward in several directions. There were few flat surfaces to the façade, which made it hard to immediately distinguish its footprint, giving off an impression of detail and complexity. Steven had read it only had twenty guest rooms, so he felt it looked much bigger than it was. It reminded him of buildings that take a lot of looking at before you understand their layout. *Whoever built it had an ego,* he thought. *It was meant to throw you off, to let you know who's boss.*

And it looks haunted.

He parked the car near the front doors. There was only one other car in the small parking lot.

Steven and Roy walked into the entryway. They stopped at the base of a beautiful staircase. A small hallway ran down the left side of it, lined with cream colored wainscoting. It had an old, classic feel. Steven noticed that it was tastefully decorated and every detail was well maintained.

A tall muscular man appeared at the end of the hallway and walked toward them. He stuck out his hand to Roy and Roy shook it. Halfway through the shake he abandoned it and pulled Roy to him, giving him a hug. Roy gave Steven a sheepish look as the man wrapped his arms around him and patted his back.

"It's so good to see you, Roy," the man said.

"You too, Pete," Roy replied. The man released him and stepped back a little.

"This is my son Steven," Roy said.

"Nice to meet you, Steven," Pete said, extending his hand. Steven half expected a hug but he didn't receive one. He was fine with that.

The sound of steps in the hallway caused all three to turn and look. Approaching was a thin woman of about thirty. The lights in the hallway were dim and the brighter lights from the kitchen beyond caused her to appear as a silhouette. As she got closer Steven could see she had beautiful features, short brown hair, and a friendly but intense stare. She was as tall as Steven and she exhibited an immediate sense of business and purpose. She walked up to Steven and extended her hand, which was thin and delicate.

"My daughter Sarah," Pete said. "Sarah, this is Roy and his son Steven."

"Welcome to you both," she said. Her voice was pleasant and welcoming, but it had a slight weariness to it, as though she'd rather be somewhere else. "Please come in," she said, motioning them into a large drawing room off the entryway.

The furniture in the room was exquisite, a mixture of antiques and modern. There was a small bar at the far end, made of polished mahogany. Very old black and white pictures lined the walls. Steven noticed the manor in several of them. They all sat.

"Nice place you have here," Steven commented. "Impressive. It looks huge from the outside."

"It is huge," Pete replied. "The house was built in the middle of the 19th century. The owners kept adding on to it over the years and eventually they wound up with more rooms than they knew what to do with. We made it a bed and breakfast when we purchased it twenty years ago." He paused. "You look good, Roy. How long has it been — six, seven years?"

"Since the fortieth reunion, you mean?" Roy asked. "About that."

"It was seeing you at the reunion that reminded me of your…" he trailed off. Pete seemed at a loss for words. Steven noticed that Sarah, sitting in a chair across from him, shifted in her seat uncomfortably.

"Ability?" Roy offered.

"Yes, ability," Pete replied, "that's what I meant. I wasn't sure what to call it."

Steven saw Sarah roll her eyes. "I take it you don't share your father's perspective of my Dad's ability?" Steven asked her. She seemed like a direct and up-front person, and Steven felt he should return the courtesy.

"I don't, no," she said. "But Pete thinks you can help us and I'm fine with anything that will help. Right now we're, well, I'll just be honest with you, we're in trouble. We have no income. Buying this place back from the people we sold it to was a big mistake."

"Now Sarah," said Pete, "we both agreed to do it." He turned to Roy. "We got if for a song!" he half laughed. "Couldn't pass it up."

"But we should have passed it up," Sarah responded. "There was a reason they sold it back to us at a loss."

Steven was a little confused. "Do you mean you sold this place to someone, and then bought it back?"

"Yes," Pete replied, "about five years ago. We'd owned it for fifteen years and it was very successful. We made good money selling it. I thought I'd retire. The new owners decided to play up a ghost angle on the place. The manor has always had stories attached to it; it's old, so how could it not? It's like a miniature version of the Winchester house, with its strange history and all.

"Well, it backfired on them. A complete mistake on their part. They lost business, and after they ran it into the ground they put it back on the market. They tried to make a profit on it, but ultimately they had to lower the price. No one wanted to buy it. Eventually it got so cheap I talked Sarah into buying it back."

"The ghost marketing was a bad idea, but that wasn't what did them in," Sarah said. "It was the deaths," she paused. "In the rooms."

"Deaths?" Roy asked.

"We never had a problem when we owned it," Pete said. "Occasionally someone had a heart attack or something, that's gonna happen over time at any hotel or place where people stay, I guarantee it. But I think in the fifteen years we owned it no one ever died here."

"But," Sarah said, "that's not what happened with the new owners. They had five deaths in five years, and all from the same thing. Word gets around. They began to lose business, and that's what caused them to sell."

"I honestly thought people would come back," Pete said. "You know, 'previous owners return the place to its former reputation', that kind of thing. I just assumed people would come back. But then we had a death here a month ago, and since then we've dropped more than fifty percent. Normally this time of year we'd be full."

"How many guests are here right now?" Steven asked.

"You're it," Pete said. "Not a single booking until two days from now. That's the trouble. These deaths have scared away business. I was hoping you could help, Roy. Use your abilities to understand what's going on here."

Roy shuffled in his seat. "Well, we'll have to see about that. What do you mean they all died from the same thing?"

"Hemorrhaging," Sarah said. "The coroner said the death was caused by some type of virus that caused them to bleed out through their skin. It was extremely gruesome - I hope to never see anything like it again. The previous deaths were the same. Keeping that kind of thing quiet isn't easy, but when it's happened five times already you can't suppress it. The staff talks, word spreads."

"Do you think it was a virus?" Steven asked.

"We had this place sanitized like you wouldn't believe," Pete said. "I suspect the previous owners did, too. Like those cruise ships with mysterious diseases. We did everything we could think of."

"Did they all die in one particular room?" Roy asked.

"No," Pete said, "all different rooms. But we had the whole place scrubbed from top to bottom when we took it over and again after the death. I don't have to tell you, we're afraid it will happen again."

Steven began to feel uncomfortable. He'd agreed to accompany his father on this trip to help out one of Roy's old friends but he wasn't aware it would involve exposure to a virus. He cleared his throat, trying to notice if it felt normal. His hands suddenly felt dirty and he wished he had some sanitizer.

"Aren't the two of you afraid you'll catch it?" Roy asked.

Sarah sighed. "That's a very good question. I suppose to some degree I am. But the thing my father and I keep coming back to is that we ran the place for fifteen years without a problem, and we seem fine now. Maybe we developed immunity to it."

"And," Pete added, "what kind of virus does that to a person? The coroner couldn't tell us exactly what the virus is, what's its name, how it's spread. They didn't identify a specific virus. They just *think* it's a virus because they don't have any better ideas."

"You think something else is going on?" Steven asked Pete.

"Yes, I do," he said emphatically, and he scrunched his red face into a frown. "From the moment we bought it back and I started walking the halls and interacting with the guests, I knew something was happening here that wasn't happening before we sold it. Something hidden. I don't know what it is, but I sense it, and I think it's responsible for all the trouble."

Sarah rolled her eyes again.

Steven and Roy looked at each other. Roy cracked a smile. Steven involuntarily smiled back.

"We'd be happy to take a look into it," Roy said.

Pete leaned back in his chair, looking up at the ceiling. When he lowered his head he had an enormous look of relief on his face. "I can't tell you how thrilled I am to hear you say that!"

"Dinner is nearly ready," Sarah said, standing. "Let's go into the kitchen and we can talk more."

◊

Dinner was served in a large ornate dining room adjacent to the kitchen. The four sat around a table designed to accommodate a dozen people, and the three other tables in the room, all of similar size, sat empty. Steven noticed a buffet table against a wall which was empty as well. Sarah had prepared dinner on four plates and Pete was liberally pouring wine. Roy and Pete talked about old school days for a while before the conversation returned to the problems in the house.

"How many rooms do you have here?" Roy asked.

"Twenty two. Nine in the south wing, eleven in the north wing, and a couple in the central part of the house. Some of them are regular rooms and some of them are suites with multiple rooms."

"It's a shame this trouble is impacting your business," Steven said. "This place is really magnificent. The grounds are beautiful. People should enjoy it here."

"They used to," Sarah said. "We were always full; many times we were running a waiting list. The skiing in the winter always kept the place full, and in the summer the lakes nearby were a huge draw. The place had a reputation."

"A damn sight better one than we have now, I'm afraid," said Pete, who had begun to show the effects of the wine.

"You mentioned earlier the place always had a reputation for ghosts?" Steven asked.

"It did," Sarah said, "but I think that's primarily due to the people who worked here. It all came from them. To this day the maids say silly things, and we just ignore them. Their talk would spread and some stories would stick. Just like the talk about the deaths."

Pete rose from the table. "That's not true!" he said dramatically. "I've got a book that'll prove you wrong!" he said, pointing a friendly finger at Sarah, and turning to stumble out of the room.

Roy, Steven, and Sarah sat in the empty dining room, hearing Pete in the distance.

"Look, you know I think this is bullshit," Sarah said. "I'm sorry to be blunt, but I'm only doing this because he insists. It's an idiotic idea. If I had my way, we'd have this place back up on the market tomorrow, even if we took a beating."

"Sorry to hear that," said Steven. "This is quite a wonderful place you've got here."

"It doesn't mean anything to me anymore," she replied. "I had it for fifteen years of my life, made a success of it. Then we sold it, moved on. I didn't want it back. That was all Pete."

"He talked you into it?" Steven asked.

"Yes," she replied, "and against my better judgment I went along with it. It was a lame idea, and I knew it. His vision of reclaiming the place was foolish."

"You don't seem like the kind of person who's a pushover," Roy said. Steven wondered if Roy was trying to get more out of her or just wanted to push her buttons. He could tell Roy didn't care much for her.

"No, I'm not," she said. "He appealed to my sense of nostalgia. He's old and he lives in the past. It clouds his judgment; I shouldn't have let it cloud mine. It was a stupid idea on his part and I should have told him so."

"And you just didn't have enough of your inner bitch turned on to say 'no'?" Roy asked.

Steven cleared his throat and turned his hand toward Roy to stop him. Then he turned to Sarah.

"You'll have to forgive him, he's a little tired from the travel."

"Nothing to forgive," Sarah said. "If my inner bitch had been turned on I definitely would have told him to go to hell. I sure wish I had. You two can walk in here and admire the place, wonder why it's a problem, whatever. But you don't have to juggle the books, try to figure out how we're going to pay the next electric bill. Pete doesn't either. He just putters around fixing things. Leaves all the hiring and firing to me, all the bookkeeping, all the taxes, mortgages, insurance, you name it. I was done with it five years ago, now I'm trapped back in it again, but worse."

Steven felt a desire to change the subject. "Are you married?" he asked her.

"With this job?" she said. "It's eighteen hours a day. No time to meet anyone."

"You're pregnant now," Roy said.

Sarah stared at him, surprised. Sarah was clearly not happy with what she had just heard. There was a long awkward pause.

"I think I'm done for the night," she said, picking up her plate. "You can bus your own plates into the kitchen." Then she walked out. Steven and Roy heard her depositing dishes into the sink.

Pete returned from another room, carrying a book in his hands. "I found it!" he said excitedly, sitting down. "Where's Sarah?"

"She's turned in for the night," Roy said.

Pete sighed. "My apologies, gentlemen. This isn't her cup of tea. I'm afraid she's pretty angry with me over the whole thing. And she's not the kind of person who believes in ghosts or psychics, or that kind of thing."

"I know how she feels," Steven said, remembering how his own skepticism had changed a few months earlier, as Roy helped him solve a similar problem at his own house. "I'm guessing she feels these deaths are all explainable in a logical and sensible way – not that it will change the bad publicity."

"That's exactly right," Pete said, agreeing with him. "I told her why I asked you down, Roy, and she came unglued. I should have warned you."

"Nah, it's no problem. They're a pain in the ass but I deal with skeptics all the time," he said, winking at Steven.

Just three months earlier Steven would have been considered more skeptical than Sarah. His home had been plagued with knockings in the middle of the night. He was convinced that he was hallucinating, hearing things and seeing violent images and scenes that his own brain was concocting. He hadn't known his father very well at the time, but Roy stepped in and helped him. Roy had a gift, something he'd suppressed the entire time Steven was growing up, but he'd recently begun to use it. Roy helped him rid his house of ghosts for good. In the process, Steven had learned to respect Roy's ability. He had gone from being a rational skeptic to being a 90% believer. There was still ten percent in the back of his mind that he didn't think would ever go away – due to habit, or more likely from fifty years of thinking a certain way.

"This book," Pete said, handing an oversized paperback to Roy, "was written about the place years ago. Sarah and I never thought much of it, but I'm convinced it's the reason the people who bought the place from us wanted to market the ghost idea. There's a lot of money to be made in ghost tours and that kind of thing. People will stay at a place just because they believe it's haunted. People make up stuff as a way to market their hotels. I'm too old school to think that was a good idea, and Sarah was too rational to have anything to do with it. But the new owners, they saw this book, read the stories, and ran with it. It worked for a while – until the deaths."

Roy handed the book to Steven without looking at it. Steven flipped it open and starting browsing. It was titled *The Ghosts of Mason Manor*. The first few chapters were about the construction of the house.

"We called the place 'Snow Meadow Bed and Breakfast' when we owned it," Pete said, "and people liked the name. But the new owners changed it back to the original name, Mason Manor, because they could leverage that book you're holding."

"You've left it Mason Manor?" Steven asked.

"Yeah," Pete replied, "I guess we should have changed it back. Now I'm glad we didn't. I'll change it back after you fix what's wrong here, Roy. That'll give us a fresh start."

Roy cleared his throat. "About that," Roy asked Pete, "I wish you would have mentioned the virus thing when we talked on the phone. That's a bit of a shock. I can understand why people don't want to stay here. I don't think I would have come down if I'd known."

"I apologize for that," Pete said. "I don't blame you for being concerned. But honestly, I don't believe that for a second. I know it's not a virus. It's something else."

"Why do you say that?" Steven asked.

"Hard to explain," Pete said. "But I knew something was wrong the first day we were in charge again. When guests would leave they looked tired, run down. When we ran the place before guests would leave rejuvenated, enthusiastic about their stay. Now they leave almost anemic. Everyone becomes crabby and unhappy. Needless to say we don't get many repeat visitors. What, is that a virus? Makes some people unhappy and kills others? Bah. And the feeling in the place has changed. I notice it at night, if I have to get up and walk the hallways for any reason. It feels wrong, not like it used to feel. I'm not sure I know how else to describe it. What could cause that?"

"Don't know yet, Pete," Roy said. "But we'll see what we can find out. What are the plans for tonight?"

"We've got a room ready for each of you," Pete said. "Sarah and I have rooms in the south wing, that's where your rooms are."

"Are these rooms where the deaths occurred?" Roy asked.

"No," Pete replied. "All those happened in the north wing."

"Do you have rooms we could take in the north wing?" Roy asked.

"Jumping right in, huh Roy?" Pete smiled.

"That's what I'm here for, Pete," Roy replied.

Two

Steven found himself in a comfortable room in the north wing with a private bathroom and a large window that offered a view of the meadow surrounding part of the manor. Above the meadow the stars were bright. *So hard to see stars in Seattle,* he thought. Here, there was no cloud cover and no ambient light. The night was dark and the stars were vivid.

He could hear Roy next door, getting situated. There was an adjoining door which he'd try in a minute after he let Roy unpack. Now he was mesmerized by the stars and he wanted to soak it in a little.

He entered the River. Steven had learned how to enter it with less pain thanks to Roy and some tricks he had taught him. The River was a moving flow, invisible to most people, but tangible and navigable if you knew how to get into it and exit it. It offered a different perspective on the world around them.

Steven had been resistant to the River when Roy first showed it to him. Roy had used it for most of his life, jumping in whenever he needed to, to help solve a problem for a friend or deal with something unusual. He'd stopped using it when he was married to Steven's mother, Claire, since she had considered it an evil practice and didn't want her boys exposed to it. Claire had tried to counter Roy's influence by taking them to church and immersing them in religious activities their entire adolescent lives, and Steven and his brother, Bernard, hated every moment of it.

Steven moved inside the River out to the meadow that surrounded the manor. From here, the stars were even more vivid, away from the lights of the house. He fell to his back and looked up. It had been a long time since he'd done this, just lay and look at the stars. Seeing them from inside the River they seemed to have color, and the longer he stared at them, the more appeared. He began to get lost in them.

Looking at the stars calmed him. When Roy had first suggested they travel from Seattle to meet with Pete, he wasn't sure he wanted to. Roy and Steven had just rid Steven's house of ghosts and Steven was exhausted from the ordeal.

He had been laid off from his job several months back. He'd been married once, but that had ended years ago. He had a son in college but rarely saw him; he was busy living his own life. So he found himself with little to do, and what he really wanted was for Roy to continue teaching him about the River. After a couple of silent nights in his cleansed house, Steven had called Roy back and said he'd go with him to southern Oregon.

Then he heard a knocking – Roy, at the adjoining door. He moved back to his room and exited the River, feeling a slice of pain in the back of his head. He had managed to reduce the effect of the pain since his first experience, when it felt as though he was being stabbed with an ice pick. Now the pain was slight and manageable. He rubbed the back of his head.

"Open up!" Roy said through the door as he banged on it. Steven walked to the adjoining door and opened it.

"It's a good thing there's not anyone else here, you'd have woken them all up," Steven said.

"You gotta check this place out!" Roy said enthusiastically. "This is *fancy*!"

Steven walked into Roy's room, and indeed, it was much nicer than Steven's room. It had a large living room with a sofa, a small kitchen with stainless steel appliances and marble countertops, and a sliding glass door that led out to a balcony. It was beautifully decorated and Steven felt jealous.

"I just have a single room with a bathroom," he said.

"Well," Roy said, "I'll let you come over and live the life of Riley if you behave yourself. Come look at this!"

Roy led Steven to the balcony and showed him a telescope on a tripod.

"Can't see anything at the moment," Roy said, "but I intend to use it in the morning."

"Probably spot some wildlife with it," Steven replied. Roy walked off the balcony and back to the kitchen.

"One thing I don't like," he said, "there's no coffee maker."

Steven followed him into the kitchen, checked the cabinets for him. "Sure there is, Dad," he said, pulling down a French press and setting it on the counter.

"What's that?" asked Roy. "It doesn't have a cord."

"It's a French press," answered Steven. "You put the coffee in, you add hot water, and press this plunger down."

"How does it stay warm?" Roy asked.

"Well," replied Steven, "it doesn't. You only make enough to drink in one sitting. I suppose you can nuke it if it gets cold."

"I don't like it," Roy said. "What's wrong with a regular coffee maker?"

"I suspect they think this is an upgrade, since you have a stove and can boil water."

"How's cold coffee an upgrade?"

Steven sighed. "I have a regular coffee maker in my room. I'll trade you."

Roy smiled. "Would you? That's a-boy."

"As long as you'll let me boil water over here when I need to."

"Why would you need to do that?" Roy asked. "I'll have regular coffee on. Just use that."

Steven moved the coffee maker from his room into Roy's kitchen and didn't bother to move the French press over to his room.

"It was nice of Pete to give you this big room," Steven said. "It will make working on things a little more comfortable. What did you think of Sarah?"

"She's nice enough for an uptight bitch," Roy replied.

Steven laughed.

"I know her type," Roy said. "Just like you, it'll take ghosts and demons coming out her ass before she'll admit they're real. Even then she'll be going on about dreaming or hallucinations. You mark my words."

Steven didn't argue. When Roy helped him rid his house of ghosts, Steven behaved the same way. He felt a little sorry for Sarah.

"Maybe we can solve what's wrong here and leave her lack of belief intact," Steven said.

"Are you sweet on her?" Roy asked.

"No!" Steven responded, surprised at the question. "She's half my age. Well, almost. I'm probably twenty years older than her."

"Been desperate since Sheryl left you," Roy said.

"Desperate?" Steven replied. "Hardly. Besides, if you're right about her being pregnant, she's got someone already."

"So you are sweet on her," Roy said. "Could you tell she was pregnant?"

"No," Steven replied. "I was surprised when you said it. How did you know?"

"The next time you're around her, see if you feel it. Concentrate on it. If your woody doesn't get in the way, that is."

Steven thought about responding to Roy's crassness, but there was little point. Roy was always crass, he wasn't going to change. Arguing with him about it would be pointless and go nowhere. And, he supposed, Sarah wasn't hard on the eyes. Her perspective on things supernatural mirrored his own recent feelings and he could relate to that. But no, he wasn't going to pursue anything with someone twenty years his junior.

"In the meantime," Steven said, "what's the plan for tonight? Do you want to stage a trance?"

"Yup, that's the plan. We can do it right here. I'll get set up, you set up to watch me."

Roy moved a chair from a small dining table into the middle of the living room. He went to his bag and removed a blindfold, which he handed to Steven. Roy sat in the chair, and Steven wrapped the blindfold loosely around Roy's head. Then Steven turned off all the lights, and sat on the sofa in the living room to watch Roy.

Steven had become accustomed to watching Roy during the trances he'd performed in his house. Roy used the blindfold to help him keep his eyes closed, and Steven knew he should not interrupt Roy until he removed the blindfold himself. In the meantime, it was Steven's job to make sure Roy stayed safe, didn't get up and walk into things or hurt himself.

They sat quietly for ten minutes. Roy was breathing steadily, and Steven was keeping an eye on him, trying to stay awake. Few things were harder to stay awake through than sitting quietly in the dark at bedtime. Steven caught himself drifting off a few times and snapped himself back to awareness. He couldn't afford to have something bad happen to Roy because he failed to do his job.

After another ten minutes, Roy spoke.

"Steven? You there?"

"Yes, I'm here," Steven replied quietly.

"I think you might like to see this," he said.

"How do I join you?" Steven asked.

"Jump in, and I'll open the trance to you," Roy replied.

"What about keeping an eye on you?" Steven asked.

"We're not going to go far."

Steven lowered his head and felt himself slip into the River. He could see Roy surrounded by a large bubble. He felt a wash of light pass over him, and he found himself inside the bubble with Roy. He could see what Roy was experiencing.

Roy was hovering over the manor, about fifty feet above the most central part of the sprawling house. As they looked down, Steven could see wisps of movement inside. They looked like large cotton balls, but they trailed some of the cotton as they moved. There were dozens and dozens of them. Some moved within a single room, others moved up and down hallways, and some moved along a repetitive pattern between rooms. Many were outside of the house, in other buildings and wandering the meadow.

What are they? Steven thought.

Ghosts, Roy answered.

Jesus, there are a lot of them, Steven thought.

More than I've ever seen in a single place before, Roy answered.

What are they doing?

Typical ghost shit, Roy answered. *Watch them for a while. We're going to pick one and try to communicate with it. Which one should we pick?*

Steven wondered if this was a test. Roy had been educating him on the gift, teaching him how to do some of the things Roy knew how to do. While Roy had experience with ghosts, Steven only knew them from the haunting at his house, and he had never interacted with one other than to be scared shitless by them. Roy operated on a whole different level with them that he'd have to learn.

He noticed one figure in the room next to his. It didn't leave the room; it just circled within it, seeming to bounce off the walls as though it was caged.

How about that one? he thought to Roy.

Good choice, Roy answered. *Let's leave the River.*

In a second, they were both back in Roy's room, with the lights still out. Steven heard Roy stand. Steven reached for a table light next to him and switched it on.

"OK, we know there's one on the other side of your room," Roy said, removing his blindfold. "We'll go talk to it."

"We couldn't do that from within the flow?" Steven asked.

"We could have gone to it, yes, but we wouldn't have been successful communicating with it," Roy answered.

"Because a ghost responds to you being physically in the room with them?" Steven asked.

"Excellent," Roy said, "you're picking it up. And you picked a perfect one, because it stays in that room for some reason. We can set up for a trance there and not have it wandering off. Really, ghosts can be incredibly stupid. Most do the same thing over and over. Makes you want to grab them and shake them and say, 'Get on with it!'"

"I'm guessing that wouldn't work," Steven said.

"If it did you would probably just piss them off," Roy said. "And it's when they become angry that you have to watch out. Stupid and angry don't blend well. They can be extremely dangerous, particularly when you're in a trance. Then again, I have met some that were unflappable, very calm no matter what you did or said."

"Any way to know in advance?" Steven asked.

"Nope," Roy said, "that's the problem with ghosts. You never know what you're going to get. You don't know until you talk to them. Let's see if we can get into that room."

Steven followed Roy out of their room and walked down the dimly lit hallway to the room on the other side of Steven's. He knocked on the door, waiting to see if someone was inside. When no reply came, he reached for the door handle and shook it.

"Of course it's locked," Roy said. "This door frame is old. We might be able to get in with a credit card. You do it." He stepped back from the door.

"Why me?" Steven asked.

"You have credit cards, right?" Roy said.

"Sure," Steven said. "You don't?"

"Don't believe in them," Roy said. "And I don't want to ruin my driver's license."

Steven stepped up to the door and removed a card from his wallet. He angled it into the door frame next to the lock and moved it up and down, trying to get the right angle. After a few moments the door popped open.

Steven walked in and turned on a light. The room was similar to Steven's, with a single bed and a connecting bathroom. Roy pulled a chair out from a desk and placed it near the foot of the bed, then he handed Steven the blindfold.

"I can't ask you in on this one," Roy said, as Steven tied the blindfold. "Too dangerous. I need you to watch me. But you can jump into the River if you want, just be ready to exit and deal with me physically if it comes to it."

"Will do," Steven said. He turned off the light and sat on the bed next to Roy.

Another fifteen minutes went by. Steven wanted to jump in and see if he could observe what was happening but he decided he'd wait until it appeared that Roy had contacted something.

Several more minutes went by silently. He felt something else in the room with them, and he turned to look at the window. A figure was there, moving slowly in front of it. It crossed back and forth a couple of times, then came closer to Steven. It stopped next to him. It was thin and faint, like a projection from a very dim bulb. He could vaguely make out feminine features. She was hunched over, as though she was crying, but there was no sound. The figure turned and looked at Roy. There seemed to be something passing between them. Steven entered the flow, and saw a woman dressed in bedclothes from another era. Her upper body shook, heaving great sobs which Steven could now hear. She was shouting things to Roy, who continued to ask her questions. The questions seemed to be making her angrier. She would turn to walk away from Roy, then turn back and shout at him. Steven couldn't make out the exact words they were saying, it was all inside the trance that Roy was projecting, but it was clearly agitating the woman. The angrier she got, the more horrifying her features became. Finally she stopped sobbing and stood still. All emotion left her face. She raised her right arm; in her hand was a revolver. At first Steven was concerned she was going to shoot Roy, but instead she brought it up to her right temple, pressed it against her head, closed her eyes, and pulled the trigger. The contents of her head hit the far wall and her body crumpled to the floor in front of Roy. Steven rushed over to the light switch and turned it on.

"Useless!" Roy said, removing his blindfold and standing up.

At first Steven was concerned Roy was talking to him in anger for having turned on the light. *He told me not to disturb him until he took off the blindfold,* he thought. *I should have listened to him.* But Steven was far too shaken by the image of the woman shooting herself to sit calmly and let the trance continue.

Roy could see the concern on Steven's face. "No, not you — her," Roy said, motioning to where the body had fallen, but was now completely gone.

"What happened?" Steven asked.

"I could only get about thirty seconds with her before she would go hysterical and blow her brains out. I went through the loop five or six times. You saw the last one. The last loop."

"You watched her shoot herself five times?" Steven asked.

"It's the only way I could talk to her. At first she would communicate. I could ask a question or two. Sometimes the answers were muddled, sometimes not. But after two or three questions, she'd start crying and ranting on and on about a guy named Benny, accusing me of turning him against her. Then, well, you saw. Then it would start again, and I'd ask a few more questions before she'd get all worked up. What a stupid bitch. I hate these kinds of ghosts, they're so self-obsessed."

"Did she say anything useful? About this place?"

"What she said was 'they come in.' That's all I could get. She's been haunting this room for eighty years. I tried to get her to tell me if anything different has happened in the past few years, but she's so wrapped up with Benny she doesn't notice much. And as you know, she never leaves this room. Something comes into the room – that's all I could get out of her."

"I could blindfold you again," Steven offered, "and see if you could get more out of her?"

"I'd rather try my luck with another one," Roy said, "than spend another minute with that stupid cow."

"All right," Steven said. "We know there was one in the hallway. Want to try there?"

"Sure," replied Roy.

They replaced the chair and left the room. Steven went into his room and retrieved a similar chair from his desk, and placed it in the middle of the hallway immediately outside his door.

"If I remember right," Steven said, "it went up and down this entire hallway, and down the steps into the lower hallway."

"I might get up and follow it," Roy said, sitting in the chair. "If I do, just follow me and make sure I don't take a tumble down stairs or anything."

"Right," Steven said, placing the blindfold on Roy.

Steven jumped into the flow earlier this time, anxious to learn from which direction the ghost would come. After several minutes, he saw the white figure materialize at the end of the hallway and begin walking toward them. As it approached he could see it was a tall man, a foot taller than Steven or Roy. He had a gaunt face with a sunken forehead. He was wearing a tuxedo, but the jacket was ripped in several places and he had blood on his shirt. Steven saw Roy begin to communicate with the figure, and it turned to face Roy, temporarily abandoning its rounds. They talked as though they had met each other on the street. Occasionally as they talked the man would glance both directions down the hallway, then return his attention to Roy. After several minutes conversing the figure reached inside his tuxedo, feeling his chest. When he pulled his hand out it was covered with blood. He turned and continued walking down the hallway. Roy did not follow him; instead he rose from the chair and removed the blindfold.

Steven dropped out of the flow, felt the familiar stab of pain in the back of his skull. He turned to Roy.

"Better?" he asked Roy.

"Much better," Roy replied. "Let's go inside, I'll tell you about it."

Three

Roy sat down in the living room and Steven went to the kitchen, hoping to find something to drink in the refrigerator. There were water bottles, and he took one for himself and Roy.

"You two were talking for a while," Steven said.

"Yeah, his name is Mr. Dennington. He insisted on exchanging names, rather a formal fellow. He talked as long as he could before he felt compelled to continue going down the hallway. But I got what I wanted – at least, as much as I was going to get."

"And what was that?" Steven asked.

"He's heard that they get invaded every night," Roy said.

"Invaded?" Steven asked. "What, the ghosts get invaded?"

"Yes, the ghosts, the whole place. Something invades, at night. He'd never seen it, just heard about it from other ghosts. You saw him, right? Did you notice the blood?"

"Yes," Steven replied.

"He'd been in some kind of altercation, he'd been stabbed. He was also drunk. He was trying to find his room. I think he appears for only a short time each night until he finds the room he's looking for. We happened to catch him in the middle of his routine."

"Twenty minutes either way and we might have missed him?" Steven asked.

"Yes," Roy said. "Ghosts like him are on a schedule. He'll always appear every night around the same time, wander the hallway looking for his room, find it, and be gone until the next night at the same time. They love their routine, won't ever give it up."

Steven thought of the ghosts that had plagued his house. "Kind of like knocking every night at 3 a.m.?"

"Exactly like that," Roy said.

"What invades the house every night? Did he know?"

"He didn't," answered Roy. "I suspect he finds his room before it happens and he's done for the night. But he'd heard about it from other ghosts."

"Why would something invade? The place is clearly haunted, isn't that enough?"

"That's a good question," said Roy. "Things often go deeper than just ghosts, as you've learned." Steven remembered what had happened at his house, months back.

Ghosts were just the start of it; the real trouble had been far worse than the ghosts. Perhaps this was similar.

"You think there's an entity like Lukas involved?" Steven asked.

"Don't know yet," said Roy. "It doesn't seem like that kind of thing, but it's too early to know."

Steven shuddered at the idea of running into Lukas, or anything like him. "What do we do next?" he asked.

"We'll try the basement next," Roy said. "He told me the ghosts down there are particularly angry about it."

"I thought you said angry ghosts aren't a good thing to be around?" Steven asked skeptically.

"If they sense we're here to help," Roy said, "there's a good chance they'll be cooperative rather than angry. After all, they're not angry at us. They're motivated."

"Unless we're walking into a trap," Steven said.

"True, ghosts can be deceptive and manipulative," Roy said. "And very dangerous. It's wise to be cautious. Still, Dennington didn't seem like the type to lie. He would have considered that discourteous."

Steven had learned to trust Roy's judgment on these types of things and he didn't press the matter further. Still, the plan sat uneasy with him. They didn't know the full scope of what they were dealing with and it wouldn't be the first time Roy had misjudged something. Steven was going to keep his radar on high.

"I need to study up on this invasion thing," Roy said. Steven knew he was referring to his book, a collection of knowledge and guidance that had been passed through their family for several generations. It was hand bound and contained multiple sections, handwritten by his father and back to his great-great grandfather. The book was almost impenetrable to Steven, but Roy had been slowly exposing pieces of it to him since their experience at Steven's house. The more he experienced, the more sense the book made to him.

"Give me an hour with the book," Roy said, "and we'll go down to the basement and see what's there."

"Dad, it's nearly 1 a.m. Pete said he was expecting us down for breakfast at 8. Are you sure you want to keep going tonight?"

"Maybe you're right," Roy said. "I'll study up for a bit, then turn in. We can hit the basement tomorrow. Probably locked anyway."

Steven wished Roy a good night and returned to his room through the adjoining door. He left it unlocked.

As he settled into bed, he grabbed *The Ghosts of Mason Manor* and read a little bit of it. The house was constructed in 1851 and was continually expanded until 1948. The original owner was Robert Maysill, an industrialist who made some money during the gold rush years. He named the house after his wife's father, a successful man who funded Maysill's initial ventures. His successors didn't fare as well in business and wound up selling the house in 1911 for what they could get for it, and since that time it passed through a series of owners. Pete and Sarah were the first to turn it into a business rather than a home.

The ghost stories in the book were typical fare – jilted brides, mothers with lost children. Steven thought about the ghost in the room next door to him, just feet from where his head now lay. It unnerved him a little, but knowing the ghost was unlikely to ever leave the room was comforting. Still, he knew she was over there, endlessly blowing her brains against the other side of the wall where Steven was sleeping. He wondered if he would hear the *splat* of it repeated throughout the night.

Stop it, he thought. *You're just giving yourself nightmares.*

He shut the book and turned off the light. He hoped Roy was doing the same, but he knew it was more likely the old man was prowling through the book, looking for answers. *He's a tough guy*, Steven thought. *Tougher than me in many ways.*

Steven's relationship with his father had changed dramatically in the past months. When they were young his overly religious mother kept him busy with church activities, and Roy always seemed out of the loop. After he grew up, he and Roy always fought, so he avoided him. It was easy to avoid his parents after he married Sheryl, though his mother always wanted to visit her grandson after he arrived. Roy had always been an enigma to him and he assumed it would always be that way.

That all changed when Steven asked Roy to help him with the knockings in his house that were keeping him up at night. He learned that there was much more to Roy than he imagined, and as they fought to rid Steven's house of ghosts they formed a new bond. Roy could be cranky and argumentative but Steven figured out how to deal with it rather than make it worse. And now he wanted to learn as much as he could from Roy. Roy said that Steven had the gift too, perhaps even stronger than Roy. It opened a whole new dimension in his life.

He slipped into the flow, and let himself drift up above the manor, looking down on it as he and Roy had done earlier in the trance. There was Roy, still reading his book at a table. Steven looked for the ghosts. He couldn't see them with the clarity that Roy had shown him in the trance, but he could still detect they were there. The ones wandering the yards and the adjacent meadow were easier to see. *Wow*, he thought. *There are so many of them, far more than the ghost book related.* He counted at least two dozen outside. *Why are they all here?*

The counting was making him drowsy. He slipped out of the flow, back in his bed. Once the pain subsided, he fell asleep and dreamed of the ghost next door.

◊

"How did you sleep?" Pete asked, filling Roy's cup of coffee at the same table they had eaten dinner at the night before.

"Not bad," Roy lied.

From Roy's tone, Pete knew that Roy was not being honest. He looked at Steven for clarification.

"You know," Steven told him, "first night in a new bed, it's always difficult."

"Yeah, I know how that goes," said Pete.

Steven didn't feel the need to relate the nightmares he had. Pete already seemed aware of the drain the place had on people. He felt sorry for Pete and didn't want to rub it in.

"Actually, it was awful," Roy corrected himself. "But part of that is my fault. I was up half the night. Steven and I did some work."

Pete looked up at Roy as though he wasn't quite ready for the news. Maybe he only half believed that Roy could help, and coming to terms with some results from Roy's work might be more frightening than what he already knew. Pete glanced into the doorway that led to the kitchen, checking for Sarah.

"You don't want her to hear this?" Steven asked.

"No, I'd rather not," Pete said. "She's already skeptical, I'm afraid this would just set her off."

"Is she out of earshot now?" Steven asked.

"I think so," Pete replied.

"I don't give a shit about that, Pete," Roy said. "Sorry, but I don't. You've got one hell of a haunted place here, but if she wants to kick us out, no problem, we'll go. I'm not gonna have my hands tied. You were the one who conveniently forgot to mention the virus to me before we drove down."

"No, no," Pete protested, "it's not like that, Roy, it really isn't. I'm just trying to keep things smooth, avoid any unnecessary confrontations. I want to hear what you found out. Go ahead, please, tell me."

"Well," Roy continued, "like I said, we did some work last night. We made contact with two of them, learned a little about what to do next."

"Which is what?" Pete said, almost in a whisper.

"We'll need access to the basement," Roy replied.

"Sure, no problem," Pete said, "I can take you down there right after breakfast." Pete looked worried. "What's in the basement?"

"Don't know yet," Roy replied, "it's just the next step. There's a lot going on here, Pete. A lot I haven't figured out yet. I'm still gathering information."

"And what information might that be?" asked Sarah, walking into the room with a plate of toast, which she sat in the middle of the table.

"I'm communicating with ghosts," Roy told her. Pete looked frozen, wondering how Sarah would respond.

"Well, isn't that interesting," Sarah said smugly. "Please do enlighten us about the spirits and spooks. Are they telling you anything?"

"They're giving us some things we can check out," Steven said, jumping in. "Hopefully we can learn more about what's going on."

Sarah turned to Steven. "Oh, so you're talking to them, too?"

"Yes," Steven replied, a little embarrassed but not willing to lie to her. "I am. At least, I watched Roy talk to them."

"Oh," she said sarcastically, "just watched. I see."

"What's the strangest thing you've seen here?" Roy asked her.

"I've never seen anything strange here," she replied.

"Now, that's not quite true Sarah," said Pete.

"It's completely true," she said.

"No, remember that once," Pete said, "I found you in the north wing scared to death. You thought you heard voices."

"It was my imagination," she protested.

"Here we go," Roy said.

"But at the time," Pete said, "I recall you insisted I check and be sure. You were terrified."

"It might have been Mr. Dennington," Steven offered. "He roams the north wing hallway at night."

Pete and Sarah placed their forks back onto their plates simultaneously. Pete looked at him, delighted. Sarah looked at him with pity.

"At least," Steven continued, "he did last night."

"Really?" Pete asked.

"He was one we made contact with," Steven said. If Roy wasn't going to fill them in, he would.

"And what did he tell you?" Pete asked.

"We need to check the basement," Roy said.

"Do you actually believe this?" Sarah asked Steven.

"Yeah, I do," Steven replied. "I saw him. In the hallway."

Sarah studied him, looking for signs of dishonesty or any crack of incredulity. He stared right back at her, almost a dare. After a moment she looked down at her plate of food.

"Well, great," she said, "so there's a ghost in the hallway. I suppose you two can get rid of it, and we'll be done with this crap."

"Not just one," Roy told her. "Hundreds. We both saw hundreds of them, in the house, in the yard, everywhere. It was like an anthill of ghosts."

Pete spilled his coffee and set his cup back on the table. Sarah cleared her throat and stood, grabbing her plate. As she turned to leave, she said to Pete, "I've had enough. You better not be paying them anything. I swear to God, if you're paying them we're going to have a problem."

"Sarah!" Pete said, rising.

"There's only one problem," Roy said. "It's not us, and it's not the ghosts. It's something else."

Pete turned to him, bracing himself for even more news. He clearly appeared at his limit. Everyone paused, waiting for Roy to explain.

"He's right," Steven offered. "The ghosts have been here for a long time, or most of them have. That's not the issue. There's something else going on."

Sarah returned her plate to the table and sat down. Steven turned to look at Roy, unsure if he should continue, if he should tell them about the 'invasion' Dennington had mentioned. Roy shook his head no, and Steven took the hint.

Sarah sighed, and held her forehead with her hand. "Listen, I'm sorry to both of you. You're guests here, and you don't deserve the way I've acted toward you. My father values your opinion. I don't want to stand in the way of that. But you have to see my side of this. If we have a virus here, it needs to be eradicated. If it's not a virus, we need to know what it is so we can rectify it and move on. There's nothing I can do about ghosts."

"But don't you see," Pete said to Sarah, "they can. Roy knows what he's doing. I need you to give them a chance."

Sarah placed her hands on either side of her plate. "You're not going to change my mind on this," she said. "I don't believe in spooks and spirits, and I'm not going to start. But I won't stand in your way. If you want to continue on with this charade, please proceed, but just leave me out of it."

"Well, that's good enough," Steven said. "We can work with that."

Sarah stood and took her plate with her as she left the room.

◊

Pete unlocked a large heavy door and swung it open, revealing a staircase leading down. He flipped a light switch and they heard the pop of a series of fluorescent lights turning on down below. "Now this is quite interesting down here. Follow me," he said and descended the wooden stairs.

The basement was extensive. It was essentially a long series of rooms that opened into each other. Parts of it were finished, others were not. As they passed from room to room it seemed as if the basement mirrored the expansion of upstairs but without any attempt to harmonize the styles of the old and new areas.

"Do people come down here much?" Steven asked.

"No, usually just me," Pete said. "I have a little workshop over there, and the furnaces and water heaters are all down here. Laundry is done upstairs, so maids never come down here. We use this place for storage – you can see there's more than enough room. Much of it is empty."

Roy began moving through the various rooms of the basement, marking them out in his mind. "Do you have a chair down here I can use?" he asked Pete. "And a flashlight?"

"Sure, right over here," Pete said, going into his workshop to retrieve them. He sat the chair in front of Roy and handed the flashlight to Steven.

"Pete," Roy said, "you're welcome to say if you want. I'm going to try and contact some of the ghosts that haunt this room. It can get a little strange and if you're at all squeamish it would be better if you went back upstairs and didn't watch."

Pete seemed excited at the opportunity, but then he hesitated as he furrowed his brow. "Is it dangerous?" he asked.

"It can be," Steven offered. "I stay awake while Roy goes into a trance. I watch him to be sure he's safe. He communicates while he's in the trance. Once he comes out of it we'll learn if he was successful. But I've seen some bizarre things while he's in the trance. You can't speak or shout out while it's going on."

Pete seemed to be going through a pros and cons list in his head. "If I go back upstairs will you tell me what happened after you're done?" Pete asked.

"Absolutely," Roy said, sitting in the chair.

"Then," Pete said, relieved, "I'll leave you to it with no interruptions from me and wait for you to come up."

"Would you turn out the light on your way up?" Steven asked.

"Sure," Pete said and turned to leave. Steven wrapped the blindfold around Roy, and after a moment the light clicked off.

Twenty minutes passed. Occasionally Steven heard a footstep overhead, but most of the time it was extremely quiet and still. *He must have the furnaces turned off,* Steven thought. When he did hear a sound, it was very different than upstairs. The multitude of connected rooms amplified some sounds while dampening others.

He let his eyes slowly adjust to the darkness of the basement. There were no windows, so it was extremely dark. Little lights from devices began to appear – the red glow of a battery recharger in the next room, the flicker of the pilot light under a nearby water heater. They cast just enough light that after several minutes he could make out the outline of Roy sitting in the chair just a few feet away.

As Roy's head started to lower to his chest, Steven entered the flow so that he would have a better view of what was going on around them. The room was suddenly much brighter. Steven turned to scan the room and was startled by a large man stumbling toward him. He was shirtless, and it looked as though pieces of his body had been hacked with a knife or large blade. His eyes were glazed over, and his mouth hung open. His teeth were rotten and green. Steven moved out of the way as the man passed by him. The man had defecated in his pants, and was streaming a trail of blood, feces and urine behind him. He stumbled another ten feet and then passed through a wall, out of sight.

Steven turned to look at Roy. He was talking to a young girl, maybe nine or ten years old. She had chains on her wrists and ankles that descended into the cement floor, secured somewhere beyond it, but she could clearly move around. Her dress looked like something from the 1960's, a short skirt and a striped top, and her hair was cut into a bob. Every now and again one of her chains would tighten, and she would become irritated and tug on it until it loosened up.

The large man emerged from the wall he had disappeared behind. This time he was dragging an axe behind him. He seemed to be walking directly at Steven. Steven knew that he was just walking a pattern that he endlessly walked, but the sight of it coming directly at him unnerved him greatly. He moved several paces to the right assuming the man would continue along his original trajectory, but the man changed direction to point directly at him again. Now he was concerned. Roy was seated about five feet away. He didn't want to disrupt Roy in his trance, and Roy didn't appear in danger, but the large man was now several paces from Steven and he was beginning to wonder how he was going to avoid him. He drifted several steps back to the left, and the man changed direction again. Steven was convinced that he was aware of him, and targeting him. He was now within a couple steps. The large man's glazed eyes cleared, and Steven saw the pupils focus on him. Then he raised the axe, and smiled, exposing his rotten teeth.

Scared and not knowing exactly what to do, Steven exited the flow, and as he felt the pain rise from his neck and into his scalp, he felt a breeze blow against his face and then swirl around his back, as though something had passed around or through him. Roy was still seated, his head thrown back. Steven decided to stay out of the flow for now. Not seeing the disturbing images the basement contained was fine with him.

After another five minutes, Roy seemed to straighten up and reached up to remove the blindfold. Steven clicked the flashlight on, shining it on the floor between them. He couldn't resist looking at the wall where the ax man had disappeared and then reemerged.

"I think we'd better go talk to Pete," Roy said standing up, "and then go back to our rooms and try to sleep. We've got more work to do and we're going to be up all night."

They walked back through several rooms and finally found the staircase. Steven followed Roy shining the light ahead for him. He was always a little worried about Roy right after he emerged from trances. Several times in the past he had been lightheaded and lost his balance. Once, he passed out. Roy seemed strong and determined though, and marched up the staircase without any hesitation.

Pete met them at the door, clearly excited to hear about the results. "How did it go?"

"Where can we talk," Roy said to him, "privately?"

Pete led them down a hallway that made several turns. It finally ended at a door that Pete unlocked with his key, and he held the door open for them to enter. Steven saw that it was a small room that could be used for a conference or meeting, containing three long tables, twenty or so chairs, and a podium with a screen behind it. "We'll be fine here," Pete said, grabbing a chair. "Sarah is on the other side of the manor."

Roy and Steven sat. Steven was as anxious to hear what Roy had to say as Pete was.

"You've got an anomaly here, Pete."

"An anomaly?" Pete asked. "What does that mean?"

"There's an event that happens every night in that basement," Roy replied. "It's unusual; it's something I've not seen before."

"Ghosts?" asked Pete.

"No, not ghosts," Roy said. "Well, yes, there's ghosts. You've got some real winners down there, let me tell you." Steven thought of the ax man – maybe Roy had seen him too. "The anomaly is something that the ghosts are drawn to. It's why you have so goddamn many of them."

Pete was enthralled by Roy's story. "What is it?" he asked breathlessly.

"I don't know yet, but the ghosts tell me that's where all the trouble is coming from. It occurs for about twenty minutes every night. When it does, I suspect it acts like a beacon to every ghost for miles in all directions. They're slowly drawn to it."

"Why would they be drawn to it?" Pete asked, becoming alarmed.

"Don't know. They might feel it holds a solution for them. Or maybe they just like how it feels. But like a moth and a lightbulb, there's nothing they can do with it when they get here. They just hover around it."

Pete narrowed his eyes and lowered his voice. "Is it what's causing the deaths?" he asked.

"I don't know," Roy said. "But we've got to figure out what it is and why it's here. I know the ghosts aren't happy about it."

"I thought you said they were drawn to it? They don't like it once they get here?" Steven asked.

"I'm guessing most of the ghosts here were drawn to this thing over many decades," Roy said. "Based on the number of ghosts we've seen I'd say it's been attracting them for a hundred years, probably more. I'm seeing some very old clothing if you know what I mean. Something changed very recently, something that angers the ghosts who are smart enough to pay attention to it."

"Maybe in the last five years, since the deaths started?" Steven asked.

"Could be," Roy replied. "Ghosts don't keep track of time very well."

"What can we do?" Pete said nervously.

"You're not going to do anything, Pete, that's why Steven and I are here," Roy said. "We have an appointment back down in the basement tonight, at 2 a.m."

"An appointment?" Pete asked.

"Yes," Roy replied. "I made an arrangement with a little girl who killed her parents decades ago. She's going to help us."

Pete's eyes went wide.

"Don't worry, Pete," Roy said, "She wants it dealt with as much as you do."

Four

Roy sat in the same chair he'd used earlier in the day. Steven had wrapped the blindfold around his head once more and stood about five feet from him with the flashlight.

"What time is it?" Roy asked.

"Ten to two," Steven answered.

"Good," Roy replied. "The little girl said it would start right at two. I'm going into the trance. Don't slip into the flow with me. See what you can see staying out here. This is all about observation. I can pick up what's inside the River, you try to detect what you can out here. We'll put it all together after it's done and see what we've got."

"Right," Steven said, and turned off his flashlight. He leaned against the wall in the room, and waited.

They didn't have to wait long. After a couple of minutes he felt a small vibration and humming sound coming from the room next door. He walked slowly over to it, taking small steps, not wanting to stumble over anything. When he reached the other room the sound was louder. It was like the sound of a refrigerator turning on, only much lower in frequency. As he approached it he could feel the vibration increase. It felt as though something was lightly shaking his skin.

He wanted to jump in the River so badly, to see what this thing might be. But he knew Roy was examining it too and Roy might not feel the vibration or hear the sound. He had his own job to do. He felt frustrated by the lack of light. He remained in the room and watched for anything unusual, waiting.

He checked his watch; it had been humming for almost ten minutes. It kept a steady rhythm. Steven sensed there were huge amounts of energy around him, performing some purpose he wasn't allowed to know. He walked back and forth in the room, trying to sense its dimensions, trying to feel when the energy increased and dissipated. In his mind he formed a circle that was about ten feet across. He kept testing the circle, wanting to ensure he had the right size to report back to Roy.

Suddenly it stopped. The vibration and humming disappeared completely. He stopped walking, waiting to see if it would come back. Instead he heard Roy standing. He flicked on his flashlight and walked back into the adjoining room to see if Roy was all right.

"What was that?" Roy asked.

"I was hoping you knew!" Steven replied. "I know it was about ten feet across, vibrating and humming in the other room."

"That's where it started," Roy said. "But it continued up the stairs, like a snake."

"If felt powerful," Steven told him, "as though there was a great deal of energy passing by me. When the humming stopped the feeling was gone."

"I have no idea what that was. I've never seen anything like it. Let' go back to our rooms," Roy said. "Now that we've experienced it, we might be able to glean something from the book."

◊

Back in their adjoining rooms in the north wing, Roy slowly turned the pages of his book, looking for sections that might explain what he just saw.

"It was like a tunnel," Roy said. "A private tunnel that had been carved out of the River. I couldn't see into it, no matter what I tried." He flipped the pages, scanning rapidly.

"Mind if I look over your shoulder?" Steven asked.

"No, go ahead," Roy said. "My eyes are tired anyway."

Steven looked at the pages of the book as Roy scanned them. Ninety percent of the writing seemed jumbled to him. The words were in English, but they made no sense. A small number of sections stood out to him; they dealt with things he had experienced while helping his dad rid his house of ghosts. When he saw writing about transformation and protection, he could understand the sentences because he had been exposed to that before. But most of it was just a blur, everything running together, making no sense at all.

After turning dozens of pages, Roy turned a last one and said, "I don't think I can keep my eyes open!"

"Wait – turn back a page," Steven said. Roy flipped the page back.

Steven scanned the page. "There – 'passage'!"

Roy quickly read the section Steven had identified. Steven picked up a few more words as he looked, but not enough to understand much more. Roy, on the other hand, seemed to be enjoying what he was reading.

"What?" Steven asked. "Tell me. What does it say?"

"It's a passageway," said Roy. "It leads somewhere a long way from here. And it's completely private."

"No way to know what's inside, or where it leads?" Steven asked.

"Nope," Roy said, reading. "That's one of its purposes, to protect the traveler inside from prying eyes."

"How is it made? Does it say?"

Roy continued reading the page. "It's constructed by someone, it isn't naturally occurring. And it takes a shitload of power to do it. I can only think of a couple of people who could pull this off."

"You know other people who do this kind of thing?" Steven asked, surprised.

Roy marked the page he was on, and flipped to a section towards the front of the book. He showed it to Steven.

"It looks like a list of names," Steven said.

"It's a directory," Roy told him. "When we meet someone, we record it. This goes back four generations, so there's a lot of names here."

Steven glanced at the bottom of the list, and he saw a name that gave him a chill: Michael. They had dealt with Michael in Seattle; Roy felt he was not a threat anymore, but Steven wasn't so sure. He was even less sure now that he saw Roy had recorded Michael's name in the book.

"Some of these people," Roy said, "could create that thing. They have the ability and the experience. But I have no idea which ones."

"Seems like we're at a dead end," Steven said.

"Not entirely," Roy replied. "We still have one more thing to check out. The end of the passageway."

"What do you mean?" Steven asked.

"Remember," Roy said, "when we were downstairs, I told you it snaked upstairs? The tunnel ends somewhere. That's where we'll catch whatever is passing through the tunnel, when it emerges from it. Tomorrow night."

"We'll have to follow it from the basement to wherever it ends?"

"Right," Roy answered. "We'll have about twenty minutes to locate the end of it, and observe what comes and goes before it shuts down and disappears."

"Let me get this straight," Steven said. "The passageway that snakes up from the basement is like a private tunnel, that keeps its occupants secret —"

"And protected!" Roy interjected.

" — and protected as they move through it. It goes from somewhere in the house down to the basement. But where does it go from there?"

"That's the power of it," Roy said. "That's why you felt the humming in that spot. That's the point where the tunnel acts as a portal. Once you pass through the basement, you wind up at the origination of the portal."

"And where is that?" Steven asked.

"I have no idea," Roy answered. "Let's figure out what's moving through it first and see where that leads us."

◊

The next morning at breakfast, Roy filled Pete in on the overnight events. Pete sat enraptured as Roy recounted the passageway in the basement and how they pieced together their next step. Roy did not mention to Pete the time they spent studying his book – Steven guessed he considered the book private, something for his and Steven's eyes only.

"It sounds like you're making progress!" Pete said. "I'm thrilled to hear it. Do you think you'll have an answer tonight?" he asked.

"Not sure," Roy said. "This stuff isn't predictable. I think we'll know more tonight. I don't think we're close to an answer yet, though."

"It's just that, well, we have guests coming tomorrow," Pete said. "There will be people in some of the rooms."

"Do you think that's wise?" Roy said. "We don't know what we're dealing with yet. It could be dangerous."

"We need the revenue," Pete said. "Sarah would flip out if I asked her not to take reservations because of what you're working on. She'd have my head!"

"Can you make sure they're in the south wing at least?" Steven asked.

"Sure, I can do that," Pete said. "It's only three rooms. The south wing can handle that easily."

"Great," Roy said. "And if we run into them in the halls or at breakfast please don't tell them what Steven and I are doing here. We're just sightseeing."

"Sure, here to take in the beauty of the place," said Pete.

"Steven and I will have another late night tonight so we're likely to sleep though most of the day today."

"No problem, I won't disturb you," Pete said.

"No Sarah this morning?" Steven asked.

"No, she's not feeling well," Pete answered. "Spent most of the morning in the bathroom, poor thing."

◊

Steven tried to read the rest of *The Ghosts of Mason Manor* but he found it slow going. Beyond the history of the place, the stories were meant to titillate readers and give them a thrill. Having seen what Steven had seen recently, the descriptions of moaning spirits and the like bored him. He would rather be reading Roy's book, but Roy was reading it himself, searching for more on portals and private passageways. Bored, he had walked the grounds of the manor, familiarizing himself with the various sections and the outer buildings. The place was huge and the way it had been expanded over the years was truly strange, with what must have been different architects and clashing styles. After his survey he took a nap and rose just before dinner.

Roy walked into his room through the adjoining doors they had agreed to leave open.

"I may have a way to trace it," Roy said. "A signature. Whoever creates this portal is likely to leave a signature. If I can detect it, we might be able to track down who is creating it."

"How will you do that?" Steven asked. "What does a signature look like?"

"I don't know for sure. It won't be on the outside of it, I'm sure of that. I'll have to look for it at the end of the tunnel, where I might be able to see the inside. Then I'll use this," Roy said, producing a round mirror.

"Wait, did you pull that off the wall in your bathroom?" Steven asked.

"Yes!" said Roy. "If there's a signature, it'll only be visible indirectly. We'll never see it staring at it normally. I'll use this once we reach the end of the tunnel to look into it and see if I can detect a pattern."

Steven frowned at Roy for ripping his bathroom apart, but inside he smiled at this news. There was a good chance that tonight's surveillance would yield some answers that they could use to shut down the portal. And just in time, with guest arriving the next day.

◊

Precisely at five minutes to two Steven and Roy turned off the flashlight in the basement and awaited the opening of the passageway. Roy had decided to not go into a trance, feeling he could detect the tunnel by just slipping into the flow. Since they would have to navigate up the stairs and who knows where from there, Steven would remain out of the River and help guide Roy through the house.

Steven waited, worried that the humming might not come again. He wondered if it appeared each night at precisely the same time. He imagined an anal retentive mastermind somewhere, obsessed with creating the portal at the exact moment every night.

After several minutes of silence, and just as Steven was beginning to fear that it would not return, the humming arrived and Steven felt his skin crawl. Roy began to walk, and Steven walked with him, turning the flashlight on and keeping it focused immediately in front of Roy's feet. Roy took small steps but there was an urgency to them. Roy's mind was in the River, and he was just mechanically moving his legs, trusting Steven to make sure he didn't walk into something or fall.

They reached the staircase and slowly marched up it, Roy in the lead, Steven keeping his hand on Roy's back, and shining the flashlight down at their feet, carefully maneuvering each stair.

At the top of the stairs, Roy turned and moved down a hallway. Steven followed. They were moving in the direction of the central rooms, where the dining room and kitchen were located. They slowly passed through each, and Steven saw Roy turn down the corridor that led to the south wing. They walked down the hallway until Roy came to a stop near a door.

"You need to see this," Roy said. "Jump in."

Steven entered the flow and immediately saw the glowing tube proceeding back down the hallway behind them. Roy was floating several feet away, further down the hall. He joined him.

What's going on? Steven thought.

Just watch, Roy replied.

Nothing happened for a moment. He kept his focus on the opening of the passageway, and after a few seconds he saw a creature emerge. It moved like an oversize, lumbering dog. It had two large eyes on the sides of its triangular head, and three stubby horns that stuck out above the eyes and its central forehead. It passed out of the tunnel, walked a short way down the hall, and passed through a wall into a room.

That's Sarah's room, Roy thought.

What do we do? Steven asked.

We watch what it does, Roy replied.

They both moved inside the room.

Sarah was sleeping in the bed; the creature approached the foot of her bed and slowly pulled the bed covering down until Sarah's body was exposed. Steven saw her pale legs and felt guilty for being in her room without her permission, seeing her exposed in this way. He began to feel that he needed to stop the creature before it could hurt her.

Do not stop it, Roy thought. *We need to see what it's going to do.*

I won't, Steven replied. *But what if it hurts her?*

This isn't the first time it's done this to her, Roy thought. *It's more important that we learn what it's doing than you be the hero.*

As they watched, the creature extended a long neck and moved its face close to Sarah's legs. A very thin black appendage unwound from a spiral inside the creature's mouth and inserted its sharp end into the flesh of her thigh. Sarah winced but did not awaken. After a few seconds, a red spot appeared on her thigh a few inches away from the proboscis. With horror Steven realized it was a pool of blood, on the surface of her skin. A second appendage shot out from the mouth of the creature and into the blood that had accumulated. After a few seconds, the pool stopped expanding, and remained the same size. Steven realized the second appendage was siphoning the blood off of Sarah's body and into the creature.

Steven looked more closely at the creature, trying to memorize it if he was given the opportunity to draw it in Roy's book. It had a hump on its back and was covered with translucent hair. The head was like an insect. It had a long tail that was twisting behind it in the same way a cat's tail will twist when it is bothered. The overall effect of it caused cognitive dissonance in Steven's mind. He imagined himself shaking his head to try and clear his brain so he could reabsorb the image, but it didn't help much. The creature was freakish. He wasn't sure he'd ever be able to draw it.

After a few minutes the proboscis was removed from her skin, the creature siphoned all remaining blood that appeared on her thigh and both appendages rolled back up into the mouth of the creature, which turned and lumbered back through the wall.

Steven and Roy followed it until it entered the passageway. As it passed into the tunnel it faded from sight. Roy exited the flow abruptly, still standing in the hallway. Steven watched as Roy held the small mirror up and aimed it at the passageway, twisting its angle to try and see into the area where the tunnel had appeared in the flow. Roy reentered the flow and observed the tunnel's reflection in the mirror his body was holding. After a few minutes, the passageway disappeared. Steven and Roy both exited the flow and stood in the hallway, as dark and as silent as it had been all night.

"It's gone now," Steven whispered to Roy, who was still looking into the mirror.

Roy held his finger up over his lips to Steven, a signal not to talk until they were somewhere more private. They passed back through the dark kitchen and dining room and walked along the silent hallways toward the north wing. Steven didn't say anything until they reached their rooms.

"What the fuck was that?" Steven said, tossing his flashlight onto a chair by the door.

"Hideous thing!" Roy said, turning to his book.

"It's obvious it was drinking her blood. What was that thing it stuck into her?"

"I suspect the first one caused the hemorrhaging," Roy said, "by injecting something into her. It probably injected a sedative or a numbing agent as well, to keep her asleep." He flipped the pages of the book, scanning for anything that might explain the creature.

"And the second thing lapped up the blood," Steven said.

"No wonder people leave here anemic," Roy said.

"Have you ever seen anything like that before?" Steven asked Roy.

"Not exactly," he answered. "It's like a mosquito in many ways."

"Except it's the size of a horse!" Steven exclaimed.

"Found it," Roy said. Steven walked over to see what Roy had found in the book. He scanned the words of the text, and they seemed to clarify as he read. Then he saw the drawing – there it was, already recorded in the book! There would be no need for him to recreate it.

"It's a type of harvester," Roy said as he read. "It collects things. Usually under the control of something or someone else."

"Someone else?" Steven asked.

"It regurgitates what it collects for the person controlling it," Roy continued reading. "It excels at being able to extract what it has been instructed to collect from other creatures without them knowing about it or being able to stop it."

"Wait," Steven said, "you're saying it doesn't eat the blood? It delivers the blood to someone else?"

"What's strange," Roy said, "is that there's nothing here about it collecting blood, or anything for that matter, from humans. It's almost exclusively used to collect matter from ghosts."

Steven thought about this. Just when he thought he'd found the cause of the problems plaguing the manor, the mystery deepened instead. Now whatever controlled the harvesters would have to be found in order to eliminate the problem.

"Why were the ghosts angry about this?" Steven asked. "It was attacking a human, do they care about that?"

"I think," Roy said still browsing, "it had been misappropriated. Re-trained to attack humans. And I think that explains the deaths."

"I'm way behind you," Steven said, shaking his head. "Start at the beginning."

Roy turned from the book. "These things are used to collect matter from ghosts, that's their main purpose. This portal is a giant ghost magnet. I think someone has been opportunistic and sent these harvesters through to collect ghost matter; after all, there's a ton of them. And I think that's why the ghosts are pissed off. I think they've been preyed on for years."

"OK, I'm with you so far," Steven said.

"But these things don't normally collect materials from humans," Roy continued, "so someone re-purposed them. Whoever was collecting ghost matter decided to collect human blood instead – or in addition. Who knows? On some nights there might be a dozen of those things emerging, some collecting from ghosts, some collecting from people. As long as they're done in twenty minutes and back in the portal before it closes, there's nothing anyone could do about it. No one would know."

"And every time the portal opens it attracts more ghosts," Steven said.

"Which in turn attracts more people," Roy said. "The previous owners actually marketed the place that way. Whoever was collecting ghost matter got greedy and decided to pick up some human matter, too."

"But why the deaths? It didn't kill Sarah."

"I think they had to train these harvesters how to collect from people," Roy said, "and some of them fucked up. They're built to collect from ghosts, not people. You can't accidentally kill a ghost. What we saw tonight was a small hemorrhage. If the harvester injected too much into their victim, instead of hemorrhaging in one spot it could cause a massive hemorrhage over the entire body. They'd never wake up, they'd bleed to death in their beds, through their skin."

There was a pause while they both thought through the idea.

"Did you see anything? In the mirror?" Steven asked.

"I saw a pattern," Roy replied. "Blue and diamond shaped. I've got a friend I can call in the morning; he should be able to tell me who is behind that pattern."

"I guess that's our next step," Steven said. "Do we tell Pete and Sarah about these creatures?"

"Let's play that by ear," Roy suggested. "I'm tired, I'm turning in for the night. I'll see you at breakfast in the morning."

"Good night, Dad," Steven said and walked into his own room. He felt exhausted as well and decided he'd get into bed, but he suspected his dreams would be clouded by the creature he saw in Sarah's room. The idea of it injecting him and collecting his blood while he slept gave him the willies. *It only comes out when the portal is open, and it isn't open right now,* he thought, allowing himself some comfort. He listened for the sound of the woman next door, preparing to shoot herself. *Perhaps she's on a timetable, too,* he thought. Based on what he had seen in her room he had the distinct impression that she was too emotional for a timetable. *I'll bet her brains hit the wall every few minutes all night long.*

He closed his eyes and tried to sleep.

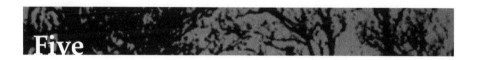

Five

Steven took another sip from his mug of coffee and dug into the omelette in front of him. It was delicious; Sarah was an excellent cook.

She sat next to him, at the head of the table. Roy and Pete sat across from each other further down.

"So I guess Pete told you we have guests arriving today," Sarah said.

"Yes, he did," answered Steven. He felt it best if he did most of the communicating with Sarah rather than Roy.

"Pete told me you two have been up at night, doing things in the basement and the hallways," she said. Pete lowered his head and stared at his food.

"Yes," Steven answered, "we've been working on a few things." He took another mouthful of food. "This is an excellent omelette, Sarah. Really stellar."

"It won't do to have other guests inconvenienced by noise in the middle of the night," she said, ignoring the compliment.

"Sarah," Pete said, "Steven and Roy are our guests too."

"Not paying guests," Sarah said. "And I don't want paying guests scared off. Things are bad enough as it is."

"Worse than bad," Roy said. "*Very* bad."

"What's that supposed to mean?" Sarah asked.

"I – we – agree with you completely," Steven jumped in. "We don't want your guests to be inconvenienced in any way." He smiled at her.

She didn't smile back, but she seemed to accept this from Steven as a gesture of goodwill.

"What they're doing," Pete said to Sarah, "is going to help us book a lot more guests in the future. We've got to get a handle on this and they're going to do it!"

"I agree we've got to get a handle on it," Sarah said, "and that's why I've got a biologist from the university coming in next week. He's an expert in rare viruses and he'll be staying for a few days, conducting his own experiments. I daresay they'll be more useful than the ones you two are doing."

"How's your leg this morning?" Roy asked. "Any pain?"

"It's fine…" Sarah said, suspiciously. "Why?"

Steven hung his head, afraid of what Roy might say next.

"Well, we observed a creature sucking blood from your leg last night," Roy said, "and I was wondering if it hurt, since he stuck something into you— " Roy stood up from the table, and jutted a finger into his thigh, a few inches below his crotch, "—right about here." His motion looked a little obscene, and Steven turned his head away in embarrassment.

Sarah turned to Steven. "You were in my room?"

Steven stammered. "Well, I,…"

She turned to Pete in a rage. "When do they go? You told me a day or two! It's been more than that! Now paying customers are coming, and I think it's time for these two charlatans – or are you perverts? – to leave."

"I suggest you stock up on iron supplements," Roy said, sitting back down. "If it does that to you every night, which it might, you're going to feel very weak."

Pete turned to Sarah, a worried look on his face. "What if they're right? Were you attacked?"

"No, of course not!" said Sarah. "They're making it up."

"You know I'm not," said Roy, sipping some coffee. "You know I'm right, don't you Sarah?"

"What were you doing in my room?" she asked. "What right do you have to be in my room, as you claim?"

"There's a portal, in the basement," Roy said.

"A portal," Sarah repeated sarcastically.

"Yes," Roy continued, "and we followed it up to the south wing. We saw a creature emerge from it and enter your room. It attacked you. It stuck something into your leg, and you began to bleed. It harvested the blood from you, then it went back into the portal."

Sarah's mouth was open. She turned again to Pete.

"Are you hearing this?" she asked him, incredulous.

"It's horrific!" Pete said.

"It's ridiculous!" Sarah snapped back. "It's delusional!" She turned to Steven and Roy. "My father doesn't have the balls to tell you this, but it's time for you two to go. Checkout time is eleven, please pack your bags and be out of here by then. And don't come back. We don't need your help."

She stood, took her plate, and left the room.

"She always leaves that way," Roy said, after she was gone.

"I'm sorry," Pete said.

"Don't be," Roy said. "We'll leave."

"But you were making such good progress," Pete said sadly. "I wish you could stay and finish."

"I'm not sure we need to stay any longer," Roy said. "Our next step will take us away from here anyway. Don't sweat it."

"What is your next step?" Pete asked.

"We've got to find out who or what is opening that portal," Roy said. "This problem isn't going to stop until we do. It has to be shut down. We have a few calls to make. I'll keep in touch with you, let you know of our progress."

Pete shook his head in appreciation. "Thank you for that. I'm sorry Sarah is so uncooperative. But rest assured I believe in both of you, in what you're doing. And we need your help, whether she knows it or not. I really do appreciate everything you've done."

"I believe you," Roy said, "but there will be more deaths if we don't put an end to it. We'll work on that. Listen, Pete, there's one thing you must do. Sarah's life is at risk. You will need to keep a sharp eye out."

"What do you mean?" Pete asked.

"There's a lot going on with her that you don't know about," Roy said. "Trust me. You've got to be vigilant. I'm going to give you something I want you to put in her room. Put it under her bed, where she won't see it or know it's there. It will help, but it won't last long. We'll do what we can from the road. But you've got to watch her closely, be prepared to take her to the hospital if she looks weak."

"OK, I will," Pete said, becoming flustered and scared.

"Great," Roy said. "We'll get packed. I'll say goodbye before we go."

Steven and Roy rose from the table and left Pete sitting, wondering what dangers he and Sarah were being left to face alone.

◊

As they packed, Steven asked Roy about what he had told Pete earlier at breakfast.

"I'll give him some protection he can put under her bed," Roy said.

"Protection? You mean the potion with booze in it? She can't have that," Steven said.

"Not a potion, an object," said Roy. "It's far less potent than the potion, and it will only last a short while, might keep that thing from her for a night or two, but then it will wear off and she'll be vulnerable again. If she wasn't so obstinate I'd have Pete dose her with protection each night, but she's too big of a know-it-all to stand for that."

"Do you think it attacks Pete, too?" Steven asked.

"It might," Roy said. "But I think the reason Sarah is in the most danger right now is the pregnancy. In some markets, blood from a pregnant woman is far more valuable than regular blood. It can be used for other purposes, more powerful recipes."

Steven and Roy finished their packing, and met with Pete in the entryway.

"Good luck," Pete said. "I'll be waiting to hear from you. You have my cell number, so don't worry about running into Sarah when you call. And my apologies for how that went this morning. She's a good girl, really. She just doesn't believe in any of this."

"You're welcome," said Roy. "We'll be in touch. And remember to keep an eye on her. Her life may depend upon it."

They all shook hands, and Steven carried his and Roy's suitcases to the car, loading them in the trunk. Roy stayed behind and handed something to Pete, which Steven assumed was the protection object. Pete and Roy chatted for a moment, then Roy joined Steven in the car, and Steven drove them down the long driveway and onto the main road. After a couple of miles they came to the intersection that would take them back to Seattle.

"Don't turn," Roy said. "Keep going straight."

"We're not going home?" Steven asked.

"Nope," Roy replied. "Is this car in good shape? Can it handle a few hundred miles?"

"Sure, it's in fine shape," Steven answered, "but why don't you tell me what you're thinking?"

"I called my friend Dixon this morning, talked with him about the pattern I saw. He's says it's from Albert, who lives in New Mexico. We need to go see him."

"That's a lot more than a few hundred miles!" Steven said. "We have to go to him? You can't just call?"

"Not with a guy like Albert," Roy said. "You talk to him in person, you don't call. I'm not sure he even has a phone."

Steven kept the car going straight, headed south. The trip would take at least a day, maybe two.

"You realize this is going to take until Thursday to get there, at least," he said to Roy.

"Not if we drive straight through. We could make it there by tomorrow morning easy. We'll switch off."

"Where at in New Mexico? Do you have his address?"

"Santa Fe."

"Of course."

"And yes, I have his address," Roy said.

Steven realized he had a supply of clothes in the trunk and there was nothing stopping them. He pressed the accelerator down and they sped toward I-5 and whatever awaited them in points south.

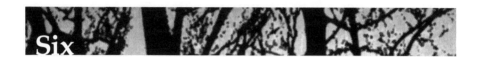

Six

Steven settled on taking I-5 south to Bakersfield, then cutting over to New Mexico via I-40. It would keep them on freeways the whole way and they could push the speed limit.

It had been years since he'd seen his father drive. Steven was worried he'd go too slow but it turned out he had the opposite problem. More than once Steven found Roy going eighty-five, ninety miles per hour. He had to talk him down.

They were blessed with good weather and made it through a couple of mountain passes without incident. They stopped the car only for gas and would use the restroom and load up with food while pumping. Before long, night settled upon them and they started switch driving every two hours. Steven found it almost impossible to sleep in the car but Roy was out the second he hit the passenger seat.

Steven looked out at the nighttime desert landscape, lit by the moon. There were not many cars or trucks on the freeway at this hour. The trip had been quiet the past several hours as

Roy slept. Steven thought about how the trip had gone so far. Roy had been a pretty good road trip companion, even if he had resisted stopping the times Steven absolutely had to. He was fairly entertaining and when they weren't sleeping he'd been explaining more about dealing with ghosts. Steven soaked it all up; he found it completely fascinating. He marveled that just a few months ago he would have considered all of this to be hogwash, just as Sarah had. But he saw and experienced too much to discount it. Now that Roy was sharing with him the combined experiences of their progenitors, Steven felt he had been let in on something special, something most people never get to experience. It excited him and he wanted to pick up as much as he could. He would quiz Roy on the things he told him and try to fully understand them. He would be the first to admit that not all of it sat well with him. Some of it disturbed him. But he listened to Roy nonetheless and gathered what he could.

As dawn slowly emerged ahead of them and Steven passed from Arizona into New Mexico, the dry desert landscape slowly changed color before his eyes. He passed by dinosaur and Native American tourist attractions without slowing. Soon he was approaching Albuquerque, where he'd switch north on I-25 to Santa Fe. He woke Roy.

"We're about an hour away," he told Roy. "Anything I need to know about this Albert fellow before we show up at his doorstep?"

"Nope," Roy replied, wiping the sleep from his eyes. "Let me do the talking. I don't want him to get pissed off and not help us out."

"Then I should do the talking," Steven said. "I don't know anyone who can make people angrier quicker than you."

"Yeah," Roy replied, "but once they discover my charm and charisma they usually come around."

Steven used the mapping information from his phone to locate the address. The sandstone pueblo architecture was a nice visual change from the green of the Northwest. They wound past art galleries, coffee shops, and signs advertising all manner of spiritual inquest and services. *Somehow I knew it would look like this,* Steven thought. "Is any of this stuff legit?" he asked Roy.

"Ten percent," Roy said. "People always believe what they want to believe. That will never change. But the ten percent, yeah, legit. Like Albert."

The voice on the GPS led them to a small brick house in a residential neighborhood. It was surrounded by other brick houses, all the same size, with no outstanding features. The neighborhood looked fifty years old. There were no signs out in front of the house offering psychic services, just a lawn with curb and gutter, like any other house on the street. Steven was disappointed; he was expecting something more grand, like a lair. This was just a suburb.

They parked the car on the street and walked to the front of the house. Roy knocked. It was opened by a small old woman.

"Hello?" she said, smiling at them over her glasses.

"Hello, I'm Roy and this is Steven. We're here to see Albert."

"Is he expecting you?" she asked in a sweet and tiny voice.

"No, I'm afraid not," Roy answered.

"I'm sorry, he doesn't take drop ins. Why don't you call him and make an appointment?" she said, starting to close the door.

"We did drive all the way from Seattle to see him," Roy said. That caused her to stop closing the door. "We drove all night, no stopping. It's urgent."

She looked at their car on the street, and saw the Washington license plates. Then she looked at Roy's face, checking him out. Then she turned to Steven, giving him the same once-over.

"Well," she said, opening the door, "if you came all that way, I suppose you had better come in."

They stepped into the entryway, both of them taking care to wipe their feet on the mat outside the door before entering.

"Why don't you both have a seat in here," she said, leading them to a living room. "I'll be right back," she said, and disappeared down a hallway.

Steven looked at Roy. "She must be his wife?"

"No," Roy replied, "that's him."

Steven shook his head in an attempt to clear it. "Him? He's a transvestite?"

"I suppose, in a way, you could say he is," Roy replied.

Albert walked into the room from the hallway, dressed in a button down shirt, tie, and slacks. He looked as if he was headed to work. He was two feet taller than the little old lady, and had brilliant white hair and a goatee that matched, very neatly trimmed. He wore round glasses that looked very old. Steven and Roy stood as he entered, and Roy shook his hand.

"Roy, and my son, Steven," Roy said, "but then, you already know that."

"Yes," said Albert, turning to shake Steven's hand. "Thank you for going along with the subterfuge. That's how I determined you were legitimate," he said smiling.

"To the neighborhood you're a little old lady," Steven said.

"An old widow who keeps to herself," he said, motioning for them to sit. "I'm going to switch to something else soon. I've been doing the old lady for so many years now, certainly some of the neighbors must wonder why she hasn't expired. It won't do to have them wondering about me."

Steven and Roy sat on a sofa opposite Albert, who sat in a large oversized chair that was obviously his favorite. Steven suspected Albert was much older than the old man he appeared to be. It felt like he was interacting with a character from a very old movie. Albert's style and language was from a bygone era.

"What can I do for you?" Albert asked. "You appear tired. Have you been travelling the whole night?"

"I got your name from Dixon," Roy said. "He helped me decipher a pattern I observed yesterday. I was hoping I could speak to you about it."

"I'd be happy to speak with you on this matter," said Albert, adjusting in his seat. "Please tell me the specifics."

Roy related the story of the manor and the passageway they'd discovered. He told him how he'd deciphered Albert's signature.

"Would you kindly pause your narrative for a moment?" Albert asked, rising from his seat and disappearing down the hallway again. Roy turned to look at Steven, they exchanged glances, but before either could speak Albert returned with a small ledger book that looked very old.

"Would you be so kind as to repeat the location?" Albert asked.

"About fifty miles east of Medford, Oregon," Roy said. "Opens at 2 a.m., lasts about twenty minutes."

Albert flipped through the pages of the book. When he reached the end of it, he flipped through it again. "Hmm, must be older than I thought," he said as he rose from his chair and went back down the hallway. He returned with another ledger, this one much older. He turned the pages with care.

"Ah, here it is," Albert said, "the Maysill contract. Paid in full into perpetuity. What are your concerns, again?"

"It creates an attraction for ghosts," Roy said.

"Yes, they always do that," Albert nodded.

"So this portal is under your control?" Steven asked.

"Yes, I oversee it. I have an assistant who handles the schedule and the execution."

"Can you tell me how long this has been going on?" Roy asked.

Albert checked the ledger. "The contract started in 1850, so approximately a hundred and sixty years, give or take a few years?"

"You mean to tell me that portal has been opening there every night for a century and a half?" Steven asked, surprised.

"Like clockwork," smiled Albert. "I always pride myself on honoring contracts to the letter. Highest quality service, that's my motto!"

"Do you have any idea how many ghosts it's attracted in that time?" Steven asked, becoming a little upset.

"I should think quite a few indeed," Albert replied.

Roy jumped in before Steven could ruin things by becoming too angry with Albert. "It seems to be functioning flawlessly," he said. "My congratulations on a job well done. Especially one that has lasted so long."

"Well," said Albert, "I do have several that predate this contract, but thank you nonetheless. I'm delighted to hear it's working out well."

"That's just it," said Steven. "It isn't working out well. We need to shut it down."

"Shut it down? That's not going to happen," Albert said, shaking his head.

"Is there any way it could be shut down?" asked Roy. "Can *you* shut it down?"

"Certainly, I could shut it down by not opening it every night," said Albert. "But I don't have that freedom. I'm under contract."

"With who?" asked Roy.

"Robert Maysill," replied Albert. "Paid in full into perpetuity."

"But Maysill is dead," said Steven, increasingly frustrated.

"I know," Albert replied. He turned to Roy. "He seems to not understand."

"He's in training, ignore him," Roy said to Albert.

"So the contract doesn't end, just because he's dead?" Steven asked.

"Why would it?" Albert said. Steven realized in an instant that this made sense. With these characters, things routinely transcended death, why shouldn't a contract?

"And he's paid you to keep opening the portal," Steven asked, "even though he's not around to use it?"

"That's correct," Albert said patiently, as though he was speaking to a small child, "he paid a fee that entitled him to an endless term, running continuously until terminated."

"But he can't terminate it, he's dead!" Steven said, exasperated.

Albert turned back to Roy. "Am I not speaking clearly?"

"I told you to ignore him," Roy said. "Do you know what Maysill used it for?"

"I do not!" Albert answered indignantly. "One of the properties of this type of portal is anonymity. It's part of what he's paying for. It's designed to be unseen, and keep its occupants hidden. I would not have even told you that Maysill was the contract holder if I did not believe your intentions were good. That and the fact I have not heard from him in over a hundred years."

"Never spied on him once or twice?" Roy asked. "Maybe took a peek, see what he was up to?"

"I'm offended you would suggest that," Albert said. "Not to mention I have approximately—" he flipped the pages of the book to illustrate his point "—two hundred or so of these portals I maintain. I don't have the time or the inclination to prowl around. And I would quickly lose my client base if I did, so I would appreciate it if you would use caution when you speak about my services."

"Forgive me," Roy replied, "I'm sure your portals are completely private in every way. I tried to examine the one we encountered in Oregon, and I assure you, I couldn't detect anything about it. Other than your signature."

"Well there you are," Albert said. "And the signature is unavoidable. But it does act as a nice piece of advertising." He smiled.

"So the only one who can end the contract is Robert Maysill," Steven said.

"Yes," Albert said. "If he terminates it, I will cease to create the portal. No one other than him. A contract is a contract."

"Of course," said Roy, "I guess our next stop is with Mr. Maysill. Thanks for your time this morning, Albert. It was a pleasure to meet you after all these years. Dixon spoke highly of you."

"Dixon is a good man," Albert said. "He's very trustworthy. If you talk to him again, give him my regards."

"Albert," Steven said, standing, "please forgive me if I've seemed ignorant. There's a lot I'm still picking up. Roy has been very patient with me but I admit sometimes I let my lack of knowledge show. I'm sorry for that."

"No need to apologize," Albert said, standing as well. "I've had trainees, I know how they think. I can tell you'll make fine progress if you keep listening to your father."

"When we find Robert," Steven said, "and get him to agree to shut down the portal, do we call you?"

"No, he needs to reach me," replied Albert. "He needs to cancel the contract directly with me."

"How will he…?" Steven stopped.

"Don't worry about it," Roy told him. "He will know how to contact Albert."

"Tell you what," Albert said, "I'll text you when it's done."

Steven was a little surprised at this. If his assumptions about Albert's age were correct, Steven just assumed he'd eschew technology.

"Give him your number, Steven," Roy said. Then he turned to Albert. "I didn't think you even had a phone. I don't do the texting thing. Or the internet."

"Oh really? I was hoping we could be Facebook friends," he said, smiling.

Seven

As they left Santa Fe, Steven peppered Roy with questions about Albert, what kind of being he was, what his true age might be, and what type of contracts he maintained. Roy answered all he could, but he didn't know much about the type of work Albert performed, just that there were people who did that type of thing and their services could be purchased. Roy felt Maysill must have paid a high price to have a contract that kept opening the portal endlessly.

As they approached Flagstaff, Steven made a case for stopping and resting for the night. They were mentally running on empty and they both needed a solid night's sleep. Roy agreed so long as their departure was early the next morning, but when it came time to leave, Roy was still sound asleep. Steven let him sleep until he woke up on his own, which was around 9 a.m. Then they piled their bags back into the car and continued back up I-40, backtracking the way they came.

"Give me your phone, will you?" Roy asked Steven. "I want to call Pete, give him an update."

Steven fished his phone out of his pocket and handed it to Roy, who thumbed through a notepad until he found Pete's number. He dialed and Pete picked up almost immediately.

"Good news, we found the guy," Roy said into the phone. Steven could hear the buzzing of Pete on the other end, asking Roy questions.

Roy filled Pete in on their visit with Albert, leaving out a good number of details like his name and the little old lady garb. They chatted for a while, then Roy hung up.

"He was surprised when I told him about the contract with Maysill," Roy told Steven. "I don't think anything like that had occurred to him."

"Maysill built the place a year after the contract started," Steven said. "I doubt the portal ran to an empty field before the house was there."

"It's all speculation until we talk to him," Roy said.

"Is that what we're going to do?" Steven asked.

"Yes," said Roy. "Pete tells me he's buried in a cemetery in Medford. We'll go there and conduct a séance."

"Not a trance?" Steven asked.

"I prefer trances when I'm dealing with ghosts," Roy said. "As far as we know, Maysill is just a corpse six feet under. It'll be easier to rouse him with a séance."

"What if we can't rouse him?" Steven asked. "What if he stays dead, or doesn't want to talk to us?"

"I think a man who had the foresight to contract out an endless portal is likely to respond to a séance. But we'll see."

They continued trading off driving and resting, stopping for gas, food and drinks. Steven was able to convince him to stop for a real meal in Bakersfield. Roy was antsy throughout the meal, wanting to get on with the trip back to Oregon. Steven distracted him by talking through how a séance would work. Once they were back on the road, they made good time and pressed on into Northern California as the day ended.

It had been about an hour since the sun set when a tire blew out and Steven pulled the car over to the side of the freeway.

"I thought you said this car could handle it?" Roy asked.

"Must have hit a nail or something," Steven replied. "The tires aren't very old."

"I hope the spare is in good shape," Roy said, getting out of the car.

Steven walked back to the trunk and opened it. He handed Roy a flashlight from an emergency kit and asked him to make sure oncoming traffic were aware of their presence while he went about changing the tire. Roy offered step-by-step advice on jacking the car, removing the lug nuts, and removing the tire. Steven let him talk. The trip had gone well so far, and he didn't want to start a fight by telling Roy he was capable of changing a tire on his own.

It was the middle of the night when they reached Medford.

"Should we go on to the manor?" Steven asked.

"No, let's just get a motel here in town," Roy said. "Our business is all here tomorrow. No sense in going out there only to have Sarah kick us out."

They drove though the main drag of town and found a motel that would work for the night.

"I'm guessing you don't want to try and find the gravesite tonight," Steven said, bringing the suitcases from the car to the room.

"There's no way I could conduct a séance right now," Roy said. "I'm beat. We've spent the last three days on the road. We'll do it tomorrow."

They settled into their rooms. Steven climbed into his bed. He was worried about Roy's stamina, but Roy showed no signs of illness or slowing. Other than being tired from the drive, he seemed fine. Steven himself was tired from the long hours on the road. He was probably being overprotective, worried when he didn't need to be.

The motel room was small by most standards, and stuffy. He got up and turned the on the air to get the circulation going. The white noise of the fan would drown out noises from the street and make it easier to get to sleep.

◊

Steven awoke to the sound of his phone ringing. He picked it up off the night stand, and saw that it was 9:00. The call was from Pete. He answered it.

"Hello?"

"Is this Steven?" It was Pete's voice.

"Yes, this is Steven. What can I do for you, Pete?"

"Are you and Roy back yet?"

"We stayed in Medford last night," Steven said. "We're at a motel."

"Thank god you didn't stay here," Pete said. "It's happened again. Another death. If you and Roy come out here right away you might make it before the cops. They're my next call."

"We're on our way," Steven said. "Try to wait as long as you can before you call the police." He hung up and walked next door to Roy's room.

Roy opened the door. "I just got a call from Pete," Steven told him. "There's been another death at the manor. We need to leave now to get there before the cops."

It was as though he'd electrified Roy, who began throwing on clothes. Within a minute they left the motel's parking lot, kicking up rocks.

When they arrived at the manor there were no ambulances or police cars outside. "We might have beat them," Steven said. They parked their car in the same spot they had used when they stayed there earlier in the week, and ran to the front door. Pete was there to meet them.

"Thanks for coming, guys. Follow me," he said, leading them down the corridor and into the south wing hallway.

"The maid found her this morning," Pete said as they approached the room.

"Where is the maid now?" asked Steven. "And where is Sarah?"

"I gave the maid the rest of the day off," Pete said. "She was hysterical, and I didn't want the other rooms to see her. I suspect she'll quit on me. Sarah has been sick all morning, she doesn't know about it yet. I wanted you to see this before she found out, otherwise you'd never get to."

Pete unlocked the door to the guest room and they all went inside. Pete closed the door behind them.

Steven brought his hand to his mouth, afraid he might vomit.

The covers of the bed had been pulled down to expose the body. *Just as the creature did to Sarah*, Steven thought. But the similarity to Sarah ended there. The woman in the bed was drenched in blood. It had soaked through all of her bed clothing, which was stuck to her like a second skin. It had seeped off the body and into the mattress. A red stain encircled the corpse at least six inches wide. The woman had defecated, and the stench was overpowering.

"We don't want to be involved with the cops," Roy said. "So let's not touch anything." He approached the woman's legs, and waved Steven over. "Look!" he said, pointing to a spot midway down her thigh.

Steven could see a small hole, about the size of the proboscis they had seen before.

"Guys, I need to place the call to the authorities," Pete said. "I don't dare wait any longer."

"Go ahead," Roy said. "We'll be done before they get here." Pete turned away and placed the call to 911.

"Why wouldn't a coroner figure out about the puncture mark?" Steven asked. "It's pretty obvious to me."

"We know where to look," Roy said. "And who knows what kind of skills the locals have."

Steven moved his hand next to the puncture wound and passed over it. "You'd better check this out, Roy," he said.

"I told you not to touch anything!" Roy said.

"No, I'm serious, watch," Steven said. As he passed his hand a few inches over the wound, the wound changed shape, twisting to match the angle of his hand. "Something's stuck in it. Should I pull it out?"

"What is he talking about?" Pete asked, hanging up from his call. "Pull out what?"

Steven wrapped his hand around something that no one in the room could see, just above the puncture wound in the woman's thigh. As he pulled it away from the body the puncture wound sealed shut. He held the invisible object up for Roy and Pete to see. Only small streaks of blood, hanging in the air inches from Steven's hand, gave the object shape.

"It broke off," Roy said. "It broke off in her."

"I can't believe it," Pete said. "Why can't I see it?"

"None of us can see it," Steven said. "It's invisible."

Pete stood looking at Roy and Steven, completely dumbfounded.

"Pete, we need to get this wrapped up and get out of here before the authorities arrive," Roy said. "Do you have a bag of some kind we could put this in?

"Yeah..." Pete said, and opened the door to leave the room. He closed the door behind him.

"So it stuck in her, and pumped into her more hemorrhaging agent than normal," Steven said.

"Or," Roy offered, "it pumped in too much agent, and when it realized its mistake, the body was so swollen it couldn't remove the proboscis. Like when you squeeze the flesh around a mosquito and it can't pull out."

"And the tunnel was closing," Steven said, "so it had no choice but to break it off and return to the passageway, or be stuck here."

"For all we know," Roy said, "it might not have made it back. It might still be in the house, waiting for it to open tomorrow. Let's get out of here. We've learned enough."

Pete returned with an oversized baggie. He held it open while Steven dropped the invisible proboscis into it, and sealed it closed.

"Can I?" asked Pete.

"Sure," said Steven, handing him the baggie. "Just don't crush it."

As they walked out of the room and back to the entryway, Pete felt the invisible prod through the baggie. "If Sarah could see this, she'd have to believe. This is incredible."

"Mind you don't stick yourself with the sharp end," Roy said.

Pete passed the baggie back to Steven, holding it by the top. "Here you go. Absolutely incredible."

Steven placed the baggie into his satchel as they rounded the corner into the entryway, where two cops were standing.

"Thank you both for staying with us," Pete said. "Please come again."

"Yes, thank you," Roy said. "Lovely place, beautiful. We'll come back. Come along Billy." He marched past the cops and out the door, with Steven following quickly.

Behind them, Pete motioned for the officers to follow him down the hall.

Eight

Steven and Roy located the gravesite for Robert Maysill in the Medford Cemetery during the daylight, knowing they would return after dusk to conduct the séance. Neither wanted to be fumbling with flashlights in the dark, looking for a headstone, potentially attracting attention. There was an above-ground Maysill crypt in a corner of the cemetery. Several Maysills were interred inside, the foremost of them, Robert.

"This is perfect," Roy said. "The cemetery closes at dusk. We'll come back when it's dark and we can do it right behind the crypt. No one will see us. We should have enough privacy to conduct a full and proper séance. Be sure to wear dark clothing."

They picked a section of the back fence that looked the most navigable as their way in later, after the gates would be closed. Then they left the cemetery.

While they were waiting for the cemetery to close, Steven tried to examine the proboscis. He could press on it through the baggie, and it felt spongy. He wondered if it could decay, like normal flesh. He stopped manhandling it and decided to try the flow instead.

He jumped into the River and picked up the baggie again. The fragment was about six inches long, thin and black, with a sharp point at the end. Where it had broken from the creature Steven could see a cross section of the material that it was composed of, which was also black. In the center it was hollow. He slipped back out of the flow, and shivered thinking of this thing invading a body, his body. Then he tried to imagine how it would feel to have your entire body bleed. *Why do I do this?* he wondered. *Why do I creep myself out like this?*

He put the baggie back down on the motel table. Roy was next door, resting, preparing for tonight. He wondered how different a séance might be from a trance. Steven had only controlled a trance once, when Roy had needed help. He wasn't sure he understood how to do it, how to manipulate it. It was completely different than slipping into the flow, which now Steven found very easy to do. It took a great deal of concentration to control a trance. Roy seemed an expert at it. It was best to let him lead the way. Roy would give him a chance when it wasn't critical.

Steven and Roy agreed they'd try the cemetery at 11 p.m. The streets of Medford were dark and the trees surrounding the cemetery made the grounds even darker. The main gates had been shut and a large chain run though its bars. They pulled the car to the back side of the cemetery at the point where they had decided they could scale the fence without attracting attention.

The trees were blowing slightly in the wind and no one was around. Everything went well until they approached the crypt. They could hear noises coming from behind it. Steven motioned for Roy to wait, and he quietly walked around the side of it. When he reached the back edge he peeked around the corner.

At first he couldn't make out the tumble of bodies on the ground. After a few seconds he recognized what he was seeing and walked back to Roy.

"Kids," Steven whispered. "I'd say he's rounding third."

"Scare 'em off," Roy whispered back. "I don't want to be here all night."

"How am I supposed to do that?" Steven asked. "Yell at them?"

"Don't yell at them, we don't want anyone to know we're here. We just want them gone."

Steven slipped into the flow and hovered over the crypt, staring down at the couple. *Sorry man, I hate to do this to you when you're so close to home base,* he thought. He moved down behind the couple and inside a large bush that blocked the view from the back fence of the cemetery. He exited the flow and shook the branches of the bush from inside it.

No reaction from the kids. They were far too engrossed in their making out to be distracted by the bush.

Steven scratched his head, thinking. *How am I supposed to do this?* He considered passing through them, but that seemed a bit perverted. While he was considering options he heard Roy think, *Oh for fuck's sake.*

Something lifted the boy up off the girl several feet in the air. The girl was irritated, then horrified as she saw him floating. He stared down at her, shrugging his shoulders, then flailing his arms, trying to grab onto something or the person he thought was behind him. When he reached about three feet above her he was moved to her side and dropped on the ground next to her. He pushed himself up off the ground and bolted for the back fence.

"Wait!" the girl cried, running after him.

Roy walked around the corner of the crypt as Steven emerged from the bush. "It'll be a story they tell their kids," Roy said, sitting down behind the crypt's back wall in a cross-legged position.

"I couldn't think of anything," Steven said, joining him. "And besides, I don't know how to do that."

"Remind me to show you, another time," Roy said, reaching out to him. "Hold my hands."

Steven reached out and grabbed Roy's hands.

"Our hands form a circle," Roy said. "No matter what happens, don't break the circle. And stay quiet unless spoken to."

Roy closed his eyes and began mumbling. After a while, Steven could tell the mumbling was actually Roy calling for Robert Mayhill, requesting him to speak. They sat like this for several minutes, Roy continuing to call. Steven's arms were beginning to grow tired, but he held them in place as Roy continued his chanting.

Another ten minutes passed before anything happened. Just as Steven was beginning to think the séance was a bust, he was shocked to see a figure materialize just outside the crypt wall. The figure was tall and lean, with a long jacket and a moustache. He hovered a few inches off the ground.

Roy spoke, his eyes still closed. "Is this Robert Maysill, the builder of Mason Manor?"

No response.

"Did you contract a portal?"

Nothing.

The figure faded from view, and reappeared next to them, sitting on the ground. Steven squeezed Roy's hand. Roy opened his eyes, looking at Steven. Steven motioned to the right. Roy turned and saw Robert Maysill sitting with them.

"Can you speak?" asked Roy.

Robert Maysill's lips moved, but neither of them could hear anything.

"Steven," said Roy, "jump in with me."

They both entered the flow. Robert Maysill's figure changed from one of dim light to a normal human being, as though he was alive and sitting next to them.

"Can you hear me?" Robert said.

"Yes," Roy replied, "we can hear you now."

"Ah, you're like Albert!" Robert said. "Most people can't do that! They just run away horrified."

"I'm Roy, and this is my son Steven. Pleased to meet you. And yes, we've been in touch with Albert."

"How is he, the old coot?"

"Same as he always is," Roy said. Roy had never met Albert before this past week, but it seemed like the right thing to say to gain Robert's confidence.

"Albert has been maintaining the portal you contracted," Roy continued. "It's still going, and we're a hundred and fifty years past your death, Robert."

"Yes, I know," Robert said. "It's wonderful. It's enticed most of the irritating folk in this graveyard over there. I have several annoying relatives who left this crypt for it decades ago. Best money I ever spent."

"Well, about that," said Roy, "I think your portal has been co-opted. Unless you were using it to harvest things."

"I certainly did!" Robert said. "I used it to harvest some of the biggest gold finds in the area. They'd open up a new mine and I'd come along after they'd collected a fair amount and take a cut for myself. They never knew where the gold went. Didn't matter how many guards they put on it. I made out like I had my own claim and was working it. But really I was lifting it off theirs!" He slapped his knee, which made no sound. "It was a lot of fun, let me tell you. And I raised enough to build that house, and set my family up for life."

"You know they had to sell the house, eventually," Roy said. "They were not good stewards of your fortune. They went bust."

"Yes, I know that," Robert said. "None of them had a head for business like me. None of them ever thought about stealing for a living!" He turned to look at Steven. *He's a sociopath,* Steven thought.

"Would you let us turn it off? The portal?" Steven asked.

"Why would I do that?" Robert asked. "It's paid for."

"Someone is using your portal to do some horrible things," Roy said.

"Like what?" Robert asked.

"Show him," Roy said to Steven. Steven broke the circle and reached into his satchel. He removed the baggie containing the section of proboscis and showed it to Robert.

"This," Roy said, pointing to the baggie, "was found in the leg of a woman this morning at the manor. A creature was trying to bleed some of her while she slept, harvest some of her blood. Instead it got this stuck in her and it caused her to hemorrhage out her skin over her whole body. She was completely covered in her own blood and died there on the bed. It's the sixth death there in the past few years."

"So?" asked Robert, unmoved.

"So," Steven said angrily, "the creature that this came from is using your portal to enter the manor and attack people. It originally attacked ghosts, harvesting matter from them. But recently it's developed a taste for human blood and it attacks the guests there every night. Most don't know they've been violated. Sometimes it screws up, like this one, and winds up killing someone."

"Your manor is the shame of the county now," Roy said. "They all think it's some kind of virus."

"What's a virus?" Robert asked.

"It's like a disease that can pass from person to person," Roy said. "They can't figure out why people in the manor die from this virus. What they're likely to do is burn the place down to try and eliminate it."

This caused Robert to be more concerned.

"That building was my life's work," he said. "It's the only thing left. It can't be burnt down. Not yet."

"Then let us shut down the portal," Roy said. "The deaths will stop, and it might salvage its reputation, spare it from the wrecking ball."

"Wrecking ball?"

"He means," said Steven, "save it from being burned down. All you have to do is tell Albert to shut it down."

Robert mulled this over. "As much as I don't want certain people back in this cemetery," he said, "I'm willing to do what you ask. But only after you do something for me, first."

"What?" asked Roy.

"There's a large amount of gold still in that house, raw gold that I lifted from the mines. I secured it in case things went south, the banks failed, that kind of thing. I landed in my grave before I needed to remove it. No one knows that it's there. I want my descendants to have it, not the people in the house now. If they burn down my house, that gold might be found by someone else. I want you to extract it and give it to Amy Maysill, no questions asked. She lives right here in Medford, visits this crypt once a month, keeps the flowers up. I doubt she has two nickels to rub together, but she still comes and keeps the front of it looking nice. You remove those bags and deliver that gold to her, I'll tell Albert to shut it down."

"Where is it? In the house?" Steven asked.

"It's in the basement. You'll have to remove bricks to get to it, and dig in a bit. It's three or four feet into the dirt. There will be a tin box, and inside it, two canvas bags filled with gold. It'll say Klamath Mining Company on the side of the bags. Get rid of the bags before you give it to her, put the gold in something else. That way she won't be questioned about it and she won't be able to say anything about where it came from."

"OK, we'll do it," said Roy.

"And gentlemen," Robert added, "don't think about taking any for yourselves. If one speck of that gold doesn't make it into Amy's hands, the deal's off."

"We understand," Steven said.

"When you give it to her," Robert said, "tell her that Patricia is fine, and asks about Mangey. Oh, and tell her more daffodils, please."

"One more thing," Roy said. "Where does the portal connect to? Where's the other end?"

"The last place I had it pointed at was a shaft of the Johnson mine, owned at the time by the Klamath Mining Company. The entrance is north of Johnson's lake, by Mount Pitt. Good luck, gentlemen. Don't trample the flowers on your way out."

With that, Robert slowly faded. Steven and Roy exited the flow and saw the last of Robert disappear as a faint glow, moving back toward the crypt wall.

Steven and Roy sat on the ground for a moment longer.

"This shouldn't be too hard," Steven said. "We talk to Pete, we go in and get the gold out of the basement, we deliver it to Amy. Simple."

"Let's get up," Roy said, attempting to stand. "My legs are cramping."

Nine

Pete had agreed to meet them at a fruit stand several miles from the manor. Steven, Roy, and Pete walked between the bushels of pears and cherries as Roy explained the situation to Pete.

"Once we find it and deliver it to her, this will be over," Roy said. "This is the solution you've been waiting for."

"But if there's gold in the house, isn't it rightfully mine, since I own the place?"

"Yes, that's true," said Roy, "but I urge you not to think that way."

"Why not?" Pete said. "If what you say is true, Sarah and I could sell the place and the gold would easily make up for our losses. We'd be set for life."

"If you do that," Roy said, "you'll be haunted by the ghost of Robert Maysill and his descendants for the rest of your life. I can guarantee that. You'll have no peace. This way, you can at least get your life back, and Sarah's too. You didn't know that gold was there before. Pretend it's just some valueless object we have to locate and deliver to someone. Don't let it tempt you."

Pete thought about this. "You're right, I'm letting greed cloud my judgment. Do you really think it's true? Can you imagine finding a bag of gold in the house? It's kind of unbelievable."

"It'll make an interesting new chapter in *The Ghosts of Mason Manor*," Steven said.

"Well," said Pete, "if we're going to remove bricks, it'll be noisy. I'll tell Sarah there's some furnace equipment I need to repair. She'll expect that to cause a racket. She monitors the front door and the common areas, but there's a side door to the basement that I can slip you in, she won't know you're there. When do you want to do it?"

"The sooner the better," said Roy. "If we can find that gold today and get it returned to his descendant in Medford, you might have a portal-free house tonight."

"And no more deaths?" asked Pete.

"No more deaths," Roy said. "Just a shitload of ghosts who'll be a lot happier. And with the portal closed, they'll eventually drift back to where they came from."

"All right," Pete said, "let's do it. Park your car out of sight and meet me at the basement door on the north side at noon. It's the door that's directly across from the gazebo. I'll let you in and we'll get started."

"Can you arrange the tools we'll need as well?" Steven asked.

"Yes, I've got everything you might need down in my workshop."

"All right then," Roy said, patting Pete on the shoulder, "we'll see you at noon and put this to rest."

Pete walked to his car and left Steven and Roy next to the flats of blueberries. As he drove off Steven asked Roy, "Do you trust him?"

"What do you mean?" Roy asked.

"I mean," Steven said as they walked to their car, "do you trust him not to bang us over our heads once we've located the gold?"

"You watch too many movies," Roy said.

◊

Steven stopped his car on the side of the road a quarter mile before the driveway to the manor and they walked the rest of the way, cutting into the woods that surround the north side of the house. As they moved from the woods through the meadow and then the property's lawn, they scanned for anyone out walking the grounds. Seeing no one, they walked past the gazebo and down three cement stairs to a large metal door that was painted light blue. They waited in the stairwell for Pete to open the door, but he didn't come.

"It's five after," Steven said, "do you think something happened to him?"

"He'll be here," Roy said, "be patient."

They waited another ten minutes, and suddenly heard the heavy door begin to move. Pete's head popped out from behind it.

"Sorry boys, I got trapped. I'm glad you waited."

Steven and Roy slipped in through the door and Pete closed and bolted it behind them.

Steven walked through the basement checking the various rooms. He stopped at the wall of one in a back corner, but he seemed perplexed.

"This is the room he told us," Steven said. "But there's no bricks here."

"What's that wall made out of?" Roy asked Pete.

"Looks like drywall to me," Pete said. "It's been drywall as long as I've been here."

"Any chance there's bricks on the other side of it?" Steven asked. "Can we cut out a section and see?"

"I don't see why not," Pete said, "I'll be right back." He left the room and returned from his workroom with a drywall saw. "Any idea where to do it?" he asked.

"Right here," Steven said, pointing to a spot about three feet off the ground. "Cut everything from here down to the floor, about three feet wide."

Pete punched a hole in the wall and began cutting. He ran into studs and had to reposition the saw, knocking out chunks of the drywall as he went. In short order they all saw red bricks behind the studs, looking very old.

"That's a good sign," said Roy.

"I'll get the pickaxe," Pete said. "Let's try to save the studs, work the bricks out around them if we can."

They took turns swinging at the bricks, and Steven began piling them in a stack in the corner of the room to keep the work area clear. Once they had knocked out six or seven bricks, Steven shined his flashlight through the hole.

"Dirt," he announced, pulling back. "This might be it. We'll need a space big enough to work a shovel into."

Pete swung his pickaxe again, knocking out more bricks. They worked at it another fifteen minutes and removed almost all the bricks in the hole.

"OK, now we dig," Roy said. "Do you have a shovel, Pete?"

Pete was breathing heavily from swinging the pickaxe. He walked into his workroom to retrieve the shovel. Steven looked at Roy.

"One of us uses the shovel, the other keeps an eye on him," Steven whispered to Roy. At first Roy was going to protest, but he thought for a moment and then shook his head in agreement.

When Pete returned with the shovel, Steven stuck out his hand to take it and Pete passed it to him. It just fit between the studs, and Steven began piling shovelfuls of dirt in another area of the room. He worked at it for several minutes, building up a sweat. He dug straight into the dirt, and after he created a hole about two feet wide and two feet deep, he expected the dirt at the top of the hole to start collapsing, but it didn't. The deeper he dug, the more he expected a collapse. Just as he was about to ask Pete and Roy to think up a way to bolster the top of the hole, his shovel hit metal.

Each of the three men in the room looked at each other. Then a smile spread to all of their faces.

Steven used the shovel to dig around the metal object, and after a few minutes he was able to dislodge it from the hole in the wall. It was a tin box, square, about a foot wide. It was heavier than he expected. He placed it down in the middle of the room.

"Open it!" Pete said. "Let's see!"

Steven pried open the tin lid of the box. Inside were two bags. Each was about the size of two fists balled together. They were both tied closed with twine. Steven removed one of the bags and held it up for the others to see.

Roy stepped up to the bag and inspected it. "'Klamath Mining Company,' just like Robert said."

"Should I untie it?" Steven asked.

"Wait," Roy said. "We need to transfer the contents to something else, as Robert instructed. Pete, could we ask you for a few more baggies like the one you gave us yesterday in the south wing?"

Pete's eyes were as wide as saucers. "Sure!" he said, and left Steven and Roy to go upstairs.

"So far so good," Roy said after he left.

"He may not try anything, but let's just be ready if he does," Steven said.

"I'm always ready," Roy said. "You're the one I worry about in that regard."

"Don't worry," Steven said. "If he tries anything, I won't second-guess myself. I'll take him down."

"Just be careful," Roy said. "Don't misjudge his actions and create a problem where none exists."

They could hear Pete coming back down the stairs. He worked his way through the basement rooms and joined them, breathing heavy. He raised his arm, holding a handful of plastic Ziploc bags.

"OK," Roy said. "Pete, can you hold open one of those bags while Steven pours the contents into it? We have to be careful and not spill any of it, or Robert will not come through for us."

Pete got down on one knee next to him as Steven untied the twine on the bag he was holding. He positioned the canvas bag over Pete's open baggie and slowly tipped it over. The contents flowed from Steven's bag into the clear baggie in Pete's hands.

"Would you look at that!" Pete said. "Sure looks like gold to me!"

They stopped and switched to a new baggie as the current one filled up. One canvas bag filled two of the Ziploc baggies. Steven shook and inspected the empty canvas bag to be sure they had emptied it completely.

They repeated the process and wound up with four Ziploc baggies full of tiny glittering nuggets. Steven placed them back into the tin box.

"Pete, do you have a way we could burn these bags?"

Pete left the room once more and returned with lighter fluid and a book of matches. He took the two bags and tossed them into the hole in the wall, then squirted a stream of fluid onto them. He lit a match and tossed it in. The bags began to burn and the smoke rose up out of the hole.

"When I refill that hole, I'll leave the ashes in there," Pete said. They watched the bags burning for a moment. "Shouldn't you two get that gold where it belongs? The sooner it's out of here the better I'll feel."

"Right," Steven said, picking up the tin box.

"I'll let you out the same door," Pete said. "Don't worry about this mess, I'll fill the hole back in and get the bricks back in place, then I'll patch the drywall. Sarah will never know."

Pete led them to the basement door and opened it for them. "Will you let me know how it goes?" he asked Roy.

"Sure," Roy said. "I'll call you as soon as we've delivered it."

"Thank you," Pete said. "I hope this settles it."

"So do I," said Roy.

Ten

Roy drove as Steven searched for Amy Maysill on his phone. He found her and mapped to her home. "She lives a few blocks from the cemetery," Steven said.

"Probably walks to it to maintain the gravesites," Roy said.

"What are we going to tell her about this?" Steven said. "I know if someone showed up at my house and said, 'Here's a shitload of gold for you,' I'd have questions."

"We'll tell her the truth," Roy replied, "but omit some parts. A recently discovered will of her ancestor disclosed the location of this treasure, and directed that it go to his descendants."

"There could be dozens of his descendants living," Steven said. "Why her?"

"She doesn't need to know this is any more than her share," Roy said.

"What if she knows other members of the family?"

"I don't know, I'll make something up," Roy said.

Steven directed Roy through a series of turns until they stopped at a small house in a run-down area. Most of the houses were poorly tended, with unmowed lawns and patches of weeds. Amy's house was the cleanest on the block; you could tell the yard was attended, and although the house was modest it looked cared-for.

"Here goes," Roy said, stopping the car on the street in front of the house. Steven removed the tin box from the trunk and they walked to the door. Roy knocked.

A short woman in her mid-thirties answered the door. She was wearing the uniform of a fast food chain. She looked tired.

"Yes?" she asked.

"Mrs. Amy Maysill?" Roy said.

She looked suspicious. "Yes, that's me."

"I'm Ben Yates and this is—" he motioned to Steven "—Henny Youngman, and we're from the law offices of your family estate. We're acting on behalf of the will of Robert Maysill, an ancestor of yours. We have an item here that you've inherited."

He really is good at this, Steven thought.

She squinted her eyes. "Inherited?"

"Yes," Roy said. "If we could come in, we'll transfer this to you. I think you'll be impressed with it."

"Are you selling something?" she said. "I have no time or money. If you pull a toaster out of that box I'll just wind up asking you to leave."

"No toaster," said Steven. "We're just delivering this. It's all yours, no sales, no strings."

She squinted her eyes further and seemed to be thinking it over. "All right, I'll let you in, but I've just finished a long shift and I'm tired, so please don't start in on a sales pitch or I'm going to kick you right out."

She opened the door and they walked inside. The living room was small but tidy. All of the furniture was dated but functional. There was a television in the corner; it was an older tube model. Steven and Roy sat on the sofa. They could feel the springs underneath the cushions.

"Thanks for letting us in," Roy said. Amy sat on a wooden chair across from them.

"So what's this about?" she asked.

"Well," started Roy, "recently the will of an ancestor of yours was discovered. It directed that certain items that had been undiscovered until just recently be given to his descendants. We researched and found you to be one of those descendants. This is your share of the items bequeathed to you. You are a descendant of Robert Maysill, correct?"

"Yes, I am," Amy said, "but his family died poor. Except for the house he built and the money he spent on a family crypt before he died, they had no money to pass on."

"That's what everyone thought," Roy said, "until this was discovered." Steven opened the box, reached in, and held up one of the baggies.

"Dirt?" she asked.

"Not dirt," Steven said. "Look closer. Here." He passed the baggie to her. It was heavier than she expected, and it fell out of her hands and to the floor. Both Steven and Roy sucked in air.

It didn't open; the seal on the baggie held. She reached down and picked it back up.

"It sure is heavy," Amy said. "What is it?"

"Gold," Roy said. "There are three more bags in this box. They're yours."

She passed the bag from one hand to the other, thinking about what they had said. Then she handed the bag back to Steven.

"Is this the part where you ask me to write a check as a good faith deposit on the gold?"

Roy chuckled. "No, we're not asking you for anything. We're going to leave this with you, free and clear. It's yours to keep, do with as you wish The only condition of the will was that it not be talked about publicly. I think your ancestor wanted it spent discreetly."

Amy sat stunned and silent. After a moment she spoke. "You're telling me that you're just giving me four bags of gold? You don't want anything?"

"That's correct," Roy said. "We don't want anything. This is an inheritance. You're entitled to it. We're merely delivering it per the directives in the will."

"I might believe you," Amy said, "if you hadn't told me his name was Henny Youngman."

They all stared at each other, waiting to see who would speak first.

"How about you tell me what's really going on?" Amy asked.

Roy sighed. "All right. You're correct, his name isn't Henny Youngman. He's my son, his name is Steven. And there isn't a will. But the rest is true. Your ancestor asked us to deliver this to you."

Amy looked at Roy. "My dead ancestor?"

"I know how this must sound," Steven said. "But Robert Maysill wanted you to have this. He directed us to it, and asked us to deliver it to you specifically. I think he's impressed with how you tend the crypt. He mentioned Patricia."

Amy brought her hand up to her mouth. She looked down at the tin box.

"I'm not going to ask how you talked with him. I just need to know if you're pulling my leg," she said, looking up at Roy and Steven, clearly perplexed. "If this is a joke, it is very cruel." She began to tear up.

"It's not a joke," Steven said. "Robert said to tell you that Patricia is fine, and asks about Mangey, whoever that is."

"Oh," Roy interjected, "and to bring more daffodils."

Amy laughed. "Mangey is what Patricia used to call our dog. I'd always call it 'the mangey old dog.' She was little and couldn't pronounce the whole thing, so she just called him 'Mangey.' The name stuck." Amy paused. "Patricia passed away years ago, when she was four. She's buried in that crypt.

I had no money to afford a plot. A man down at city parks found out I could use the crypt for free, since there were spaces still open in it and I was in the family. I'd go down there to talk to her. You can walk into it, there's a bench inside. I'd sit there and just talk. Sometimes I'd look over the names on the other graves and talk to them too. Just casual, funny stuff, asking them if they were taking good care of her, that kind of thing. I didn't mean anything by it. I didn't think they were listening."

They sat in silence for a moment.

"So this is for real?" Amy said, looking up at Roy and Steven.

"Yes," said Roy. "When we leave, this gold stays here, with you. It's all yours."

"My advice is not to tell anyone you have it," Steven said. "No one, until you can take it somewhere and get it exchanged for cash," Steven said. "If you decide to keep any of it, I suggest getting a safe deposit box at your bank."

"I've never had anything like a safe deposit box. How much do you think it's worth?" she asked.

"Based on its weight and the price of gold," Steven said, "I'd say hundreds of thousands of dollars."

Amy slowly grabbed the sides of her head with her hands and stared at the floor. She seemed to be holding her head together, as though it might explode at any moment. When she raised her head to look at Steven and Roy there were tears on her cheeks.

"Well I don't know what to say," she said. "I'm...numb."

"The main thing," Roy said, "is to take proper care of this. Don't tell anyone, not even people you trust. Go down to the bank today and lock it up until you decide what to do with it. We're going to go now. Steven will leave you his number in case you need us for anything."

"Do you have a pen?" Steven asked.

They all stood and Steven and Amy exchanged phone numbers. They walked to the door.

"You realize this completely changes everything, for me, for my kids?" Amy asked as they walked out the door and turned to face her in the doorway. "I have three boys, all in school. No husband. I work two jobs most days. We barely get by. Now…"

"I think that's what Robert had in mind," Roy told her.

"Thank you," she said.

"You're welcome," they both said, and turned to walk to their car. Amy watched them as they got in and drove off. Then she closed the door and turned to the tin box on her living room floor that had just altered the course of her life.

◊

Steven and Roy drove back to their motel. They were both a little overwhelmed by the experience with Amy.

"I told you sometimes good things happen," Roy said. "This is one of those times."

"I hope she spends it well," Steven said. "When people win the lottery and suddenly come into a lot of money, you wonder if they will go crazy and lose it all."

"I don't think that will happen with her," Roy said. "It's not millions. It's enough for her to pay off a mortgage and put her boys through college, but she'll still work. It'll just be a lot easier."

Once they entered the motel, Steven walked into Roy's room.

"No text from Albert yet," Steven said, checking his phone. "Is there anything we should do?"

"Just wait," Roy said. "It'll come. We did exactly what he asked. If it doesn't, we'll go back to the cemetery and have another conversation with him."

"I'll be next door," Steven said. "If the text comes through, I'll let you know."

Steven walked over to his room and laid down on the bed. He was pleased at how things had gone with the day. Pete had been cooperative during the digging and giving Amy the gold had been a rare experience. *It's not every day you get to change someone's life like that,* he thought. *Now all we need is that text from Albert.*

As though thinking about it caused it, Steven's phone buzzed. He checked it and walked over to Roy's.

"You're right," he said to Roy, "it came through. 'Instructed by RM to close it permanently effective immediately' it says."

"Ha ha!" Roy said, clapping his hands together. "I think that will do it. Let's call Pete and give him the good news!"

Steven dialed the phone and handed it to Roy. Roy spoke with Pete and explained about the gold delivery to Amy and the text from Albert. They discussed a few other things. Roy assured him things would start to improve at the manor, starting tonight.

When he hung up, Steven asked him if Pete seemed OK.

"He's ecstatic," Roy told him. "He said we're welcome as guests at the manor anytime, no charge. Let's celebrate! Maybe we can find a nice steak place here in town."

"What, you don't want to head back to Seattle?" Steven asked.

"No, let's stay the night and go back in the morning," Roy said. "What I'd really like is a big fat steak and a bottle of wine to go with it. Does that fancy phone of yours have all the steak places in it?"

Steven smiled and went to work checking out reviews.

◊

Steven and Roy spared no expense at dinner that night. They started off toasting each other with whiskey. Each ordered their fill of meat and side dishes. They split a bottle of wine between the two of them. By the time they got back to their motel they were ready to sleep. They wished each other good night and settled in for the night.

Steven was awakened by his phone. As he picked it up to see who was calling, he checked the time: 3 a.m. The call was from Pete.

"Hello?" Steven said groggily. "Pete?"

"Steven, are you still in town? Can you come out here right away?" Steven could hear panic in Pete's voice.

"What's wrong?" he asked.

"Everything's gone to hell," Pete replied. "Sarah has barricaded herself in her room, the guests are packing up and leaving, and..." he paused, "...well, I guess you should see it. Can you and Roy come out here, now? I don't know where else to turn. Roy said things would be better, but the exact opposite is happening. We need help!"

"We'll be right there," Steven said, and hung up the phone. He threw on some clothes and went next door to rouse Roy.

Eleven

"Maybe we've been double crossed," said Steven as he drove out to the manor. "Robert, or Albert."

"Robert, maybe," Roy said. "Albert definitely not. If he said he shut down the portal, I believe him."

"Maybe the ghosts aren't happy about it being shut down," Steven suggested. "Maybe they're not going to just drift away quietly. Or maybe it has to do with the removal of the gold."

"If I had a dollar for every one of your maybes," Roy said, "we'd be shittin' in knee high cotton. Why don't we just wait and see what Pete is talking about."

That silenced Steven. He could tell Roy was pissed that things hadn't gone as he'd promised to Pete. Roy had miscalculated something, and Steven realized he was just irritating him with scenarios. Steven was much more of a worrier, a planner. He liked to think things through, run options in his mind. Roy was more able to take things as they came.

They drove the remaining distance in silence, and in the dark. The sun wouldn't rise for another couple of hours. As Steven pulled the car into the long driveway that led to the house, both he and Roy could see something was wrong.

"Look at that!" Roy said.

Steven slowly inched the car along the driveway towards the house, a thousand feet in the distance. Lights were on in the central common rooms. As they watched, a light would flash behind a window in the guest rooms, as though someone had flashed a camera in a darkened room. Then another flash would come from another window. The house would sit dark for a moment, then another flash would come.

"Do you want to check this out, before we meet Pete?" Steven asked.

Roy slipped into the River and observed the house from within the flow. Everything looked normal, as it had on the first night they were there. He could see the wisps of ghosts moving within the house and in the yard, but they didn't seem to be moving any differently than before. He moved to a position above the house, the same angle he had shown Steven on the first night. The ghosts were moving in the same patterns, some confined to a single room, others moving between them. He saw the woman in the room next to Steven's — she was walking back and forth, preparing to shoot herself. He looked for the little girl and found her in the basement, chained near the furnace. She was yanking on the chains just as before. He looked around for any other disturbances, any beings other than ghosts. He didn't see any, but that didn't mean they weren't there.

He exited the flow. "The ghosts all look the same," he told Steven. "They're doing the same things they were doing when we were here before. I don't see anything else."

"No portal?" Steven asked.

"None," Roy answered, "but then it's past the time it would have appeared, if it had. I doubt it did."

Steven pulled the car in front of the house, and they both left it and walked to the main door. Pete was there to meet them.

"I thought you said it would be over!" Pete said to Roy.

"The portal is closed Pete, I'm sure of that," Roy told him.

"Then how do you explain this?" Pete said.

"Explain what?" Steven asked.

Pete pointed to the drawing room where they had first met Sarah. Roy and Steven walked into the room and glanced around.

On the floor was a man twisting in pain, dressed in old clothes. After a moment, another man materialized above him, straddling him with both legs. He held a revolver and he raised it to point at the lying man. Then he pulled the trigger repeatedly, firing bullet after bullet into the man's head. After the third bullet the man's head split apart, blood spreading on the floor. He continued firing until he had emptied his revolver. Then he looked up at Steven, Roy and Pete, standing in the entryway to the room. He opened the revolver and dumped the shells on the floor. Then he started reloading it.

"He will come after you," Pete said, "if you don't leave the room. He thinks we're witnesses."

They all hurried into the main hallway at the base of the stairs. "We're safe out here," Pete said. "He doesn't leave that room."

Steven noticed a lady in an exquisite dress descending the staircase. She was regal and refined, with excellent posture and a highly held chin. When she reached the bottom of the stairs, she turned, and walked toward them.

Steven instinctually stepped to the side to allow her to pass, and Pete went with him. But Roy stood still as the woman passed through him and continued into the corridor towards the kitchen.

"It's like this all over the house," Pete said.

"We saw flashing in the windows as we drove up," Steven said. "Do you know what that is?"

"One of the guests," Pete said. "He's trying to take pictures of them. All the other guests left. Scared to death, in the middle of the night. They just packed up and took off. Sarah's been in her bedroom all night, she won't come out."

They heard gunshots coming from the drawing room as the ghost reenacted the murder they had just witnessed.

"Every couple of minutes," Pete said, "six gunshots. Goes on and on."

"Pete, take us down to the basement," said Roy. "I want to see if the portal is still there."

They walked to the door that led down to the basement. Pete unlocked it and opened it. He reached to turn on the stairwell light, but before he could reach it, he glanced at the bottom of the stairs. There was a man barely visible, sitting on the bottom step, with his back to them. As Pete turned on the light, the man twisted his neck around to face them. His face was missing as though it had been sheared off by a blade.

"I'm not going down there," Pete said. "Sorry guys, I can't do it."

"I suggest we ride this out until daylight," Roy said. "We know our two rooms in the north wing are ghost free. Is yours?" he asked Pete.

"What?" asked Pete.

"The room you sleep in, Pete. Were there ghosts in it?" Roy repeated.

"No," he answered, "not that I saw. I heard the gunshots and I got up. That's when I saw all of this."

"I suspect Sarah's room is ghost free too," Roy said, "or she wouldn't still be in there. Can Steven and I return to our rooms in the north wing for the rest of the night? I think once daylight hits we'll see things calm down enough that we can go down into the basement."

"Yes," Pete said, pulling a keychain out of his pocket and sliding a key off it. "Your rooms are still open, you can use them. This is a master key."

"Go to your room, Pete," Roy said. "Stay there. Put in ear plugs if you have to. Let's meet in the dining room at 7 a.m. It'll be light then, and we can talk this through without all this…" he waved his hand dismissively, "…hubbub."

"Right," Pete said, and turned to walk off to his room. Steven and Roy made their way to the north wing to find their rooms.

◊

"Be sure to throw the chain on your door," Steven suggested once they were inside their original rooms. "We don't want the photographer walking in on us."

"Good idea!" Roy said, chaining his door.

The rooms had been cleaned and made up. Neither Steven or Roy had any clothes or toiletries with them, they were all back at the motel. They would have to make do with the clothes on their backs until they could go back into town.

Steven walked through the adjoining door into Roy's room. "What do you think?" Steven asked.

"I don't think anything out of the ordinary is happening here," Roy said, "except they're visible. We already knew this was a ghost trap, they're here by the hundreds. For some reason, once the portal shut down they became visible. Or at least some of them did."

"Pete looked terrified," Steven said. "He was scared out of his mind."

"Of course he is," Roy said. "What he doesn't realize is these ghosts are always behaving this way, doing these things. He just never sees it. They're just doing what they always do every night."

"Why would they become visible?" Steven asked. "Did something about the portal malfunction? Are they angry, is that why they're showing themselves?"

"I doubt it," Roy said. "Only a few of the ghosts here actually have enough strength to become visible over the years, and even then only for brief moments. That's where the material for the ghost book Pete gave you comes from – people who caught glimpses of the few that had enough strength to manifest. To see so many of them visible, all at once, I don't think this is the ghosts' doing. Or the portal. This took a lot of energy."

"Then what?" Steven asked.

"I wonder if that mirror is still available," Roy said, walking into his bathroom. "Ah! Here it is." He returned with the mirror he had used to detect the pattern in the tunnel.

"Here, hold this, will you?" he said, handing the mirror to Steven. "I'm going in the River. Just stand and hold it, just like that. Don't move it."

Steven held the mirror while Roy slipped into the flow. After a minute, he returned.

"That motherfucker!" Roy said as he emerged from the River. "You can put the mirror down."

"What?" Steven asked. "What did you see?"

"A pattern. This one I already recognize. It's descended around the house and yard."

"What's descended?" Steven asked.

"It's like a curse," Roy answered. "Fresh, just cast. Makes the ghosts visible to human eyes. It'll last until dawn, then the sun will eliminate it. I've seen the pattern before. A little ratfuck named Jurgen. He's a low-life scumball."

"He's casting a curse on the house? Why?"

"He's an asshole," said Roy, becoming angry. "It's just the kind of thing he'd do, the little fucker."

"Tell me what's going on!" Steven raised his voice to Roy. "Stop and explain it to me!"

Roy sat down on the sofa in the living room of the suite. "Jurgen is the lowest of the low. He'll sell anything to make a buck. He steals most of what he sells, and he's not above selling the worst stuff, the most degenerate things." A light clicked on in Roy's head. He turned to face Steven, smiling broadly. "Including ghost matter. And human blood! He's been the one on the other end of the portal! He's pissed!" Roy was delighted with his discovery.

"Will you please let me in on what you've figured out?" Steven said. "I feel really in the dark here."

"Robert didn't have a chance to close the portal before he died, right? He left it open, paid for into eternity. It's been sitting here, attracting ghosts for a hundred and seventy years."

"Right," nodded Steven.

"So, along comes an opportunistic fuck like Jurgen. He discovers the portal. He must have found the other end inside the mine Robert mentioned. It's just like him to be prowling around an abandoned mine, looking for things he could sell. He had to be there in the middle of the night, right when the portal opened. He recognized what it was, and he went through it, finding himself in the basement of the manor – surrounded by a mother lode of ghosts."

"OK, I'm with you," Steven said.

"Jurgen is a scavenger. He collects things and refines them into other materials that he can sell. Mostly recipe components. You can get the basic stuff from him, but he specializes in exotic items, stuff that's hard to get. Sells for more money."

"Like ghost matter?"

"Exactly!" Roy agreed. "Ghost matter isn't easy to come by. Here he's found a free, abandoned, secret passageway to a bonanza of ghost matter. He realizes he just needs to send through a few trained harvesters when the portal is open, and he's got an ongoing supply of ghost matter to sell or refine. Right up his alley."

"And that's why the ghosts were upset about it," Steven said. "They didn't like being harvested."

"Yes, but not enough to leave, apparently," Roy said. "The draw of the portal was too strong to resist even if it cost them some matter some nights."

"But the deaths? Harvesters gone wrong?"

"In addition to an endless supply of ghosts, Jurgen realizes he's also got a steady supply of sleeping humans. He crosses a line, repurposes some harvesters to collect blood, and sends them through the tunnel. It's risky since harvesters aren't used that way, but we know that's what's happening, we saw it ourselves. Human blood is worth a lot as a compound. Some blood is worth much more, like the blood of a pregnant woman. The portal gave him a nice income stream."

"Before we shut it down," Steven said.

"Yes," Roy agreed, "before we shut it down. Now he's lost his easy supply of bodies and ghosts. He's pissed. He probably thinks he can get us to reopen it by scaring the daylights out of whoever did it. That won't work with us of course."

"But it's scaring the daylights out of Pete and Sarah," Steven said, "and their guests. Can we reopen it? The portal?"

"No way," Roy said. "You have to pay someone like Albert to do it, and neither of us could afford it, trust me. Not to mention we'd be opening the place back up to the harvesters. No, that's not the solution."

"What do we do? We can't leave them like this."

"Jurgen is a vengeful little fucker," Roy said. "I dealt with him once before, when a friend was after some unusual ingredients. He tried to screw us over, but we caught him and forced him to be equitable. Really pissed him off. He tormented us about it until we stood up to him, showed him we wouldn't be bullied, then he backed down. He's a despicable person. I was hoping I'd never run into him again."

Roy got up and began pacing the room.

"In this case," Roy continued, "he probably wants to know who turned off his supply line. The curse is to shake us out. It only lasts a night, he'll have to re-cast it every night. He'll never find out who did it, or if he does, he'll believe it was Robert Maysill who shut it down. He had it good while it lasted, now it's over. Eventually he'll get tired and give up, move on."

"How long might that take?" Steven said. "I don't think Pete and Sarah can go through much more of this."

"What they should do," Roy answered, "is leverage it. They'd have tourists coming from miles around if someone published proof that it is still haunted. Get those TV reality shows out here. Take advantage of it until Jurgen drops the curse, or the ghosts drift away. Or both. It costs Jurgen every time he casts it, and if Jurgen saw them making money off it, he'd drop it in a heartbeat. He's a jealous little fucker, very petty."

"Sarah won't do that," Steven said. "You know she won't."

"Yeah," Roy replied, "she is an obstinate one. I'll bet even with ghosts chasing her down the hallways she's insisting they're hallucinations. Probably wants Pete to take her to the hospital in Medford to get checked out. She'll figure it out eventually."

"You told them this would solve it," Steven said. "Pete was counting on you."

Roy stopped pacing and turned to look at Steven. "Don't you lay a guilt trip on me," Roy said, pointing his finger at him. "Things don't always go as planned in this business. We did what we thought would solve it. It will, if they give it time."

"You know that's not going to work," Steven said. "They're terrified, they're not thinking about selling tickets to it."

"Well, what do you propose, then?" Roy said, exasperated.

"We find Jurgen and confront him," Steven said. "We get him to drop the curse. That's all that needs to happen, right?"

"Oh, we just get him to drop it," Roy said sarcastically.

"Yes, he drops it, the ghosts become invisible again, problem solved. They eventually drift back to where they came from. Pete and Sarah can start over here, try to rebuild their business. And you can tell Pete you solved it."

"I did solve it," Roy snapped at Steven.

"Not good enough!" Steven shouted back at him. Then he lowered his voice. "Not good enough."

Roy stomped off to the bathroom, sulking. He slammed the door closed.

Steven walked back to his room and laid down on the bed. This reminded him of when he and his father would fight as he was growing up. It had always been easy to fight with Roy, and Steven knew all the buttons to push. Over the years Steven had learned how to avoid the fights, when to drop things that might erupt. But in this case he had heard Roy's promises to Pete. He had told him to trust him. He had assured him. Pete had done everything they asked him to do. They had done a lot to help Pete, but they hadn't done enough. Leaving it like this would be like leaving a rabid dog loose in a playground. It wasn't acceptable. Steven wasn't going to let Roy call it a day and go home.

Twelve

Steven and Roy walked down to meet Pete separately the next morning. Steven was still angry with Roy for thinking they could just let things stand and sort themselves out, and they hadn't spoken to each other since their fight the night before.

Steven joined Pete at the breakfast table. "Things appear to have quieted down," Steven said.

"Indeed," Pete said. "The gunshots stopped as the sun came up, just like Roy said."

It was obvious Pete still had faith in Roy. If Steven had any say in the matter, he'd make sure Pete's faith wasn't misplaced.

Pete was picking at a muffin and drinking coffee. He handed a basket of muffins to Steven. "Didn't feel much like cooking this morning," Pete said.

"I understand," Steven said. "Is the guest who was taking the pictures still here?"

"He left after they all disappeared," Pete said. "Told me he had to be back in Portland today, but that he was coming back with some friends next week."

"Well, that's a good sign at least," Steven said. Pete shot him a look that told him he did *not* think it was a good sign.

"Is Sarah OK?" Steven asked.

"Yes," Pete answered, "she's up. I'm expecting her this morning, don't know right where she is at the moment."

Roy entered the room. He walked to a place at the table and sat. Pete offered him the coffee pot and Steven passed him the basket of muffins.

Steven looked at Pete. He could tell Pete sensed something was up between him and Roy. They weren't looking at each other or acknowledging each other. *He's probably wondering what happened last night after we left him*, Steven thought.

"Pete, I think I know what's causing this trouble," Roy said. "At least, causing what you saw last night."

Pete looked down at his plate and took another sip of coffee. He didn't say anything.

"Pete," Roy said, "the portal is closed. We can go downstairs and check, but I'm sure of it. What's happening now is something else."

"And what is that?" Pete asked.

"Are you sure you want me to tell you?" Roy asked.

"Yes, Mr. Hall," Sarah said, entering the room from the kitchen and sitting at the table. "We'd like to know." She turned to Steven. "Would you pass the coffee?"

"I think," said Roy, "that you might find it a little hard to believe."

"After last night," Sarah said, pouring herself a cup, "I doubt I'd find anything hard to believe. If you have an answer, I'm all ears."

Roy cleared his throat. "Well, what you saw last night goes on here all the time, all night long. Every night. You just can't see it. Remember when I told you at that first breakfast that there were hundreds of ghosts here? Well, it's true. You can't see them normally. Last night you could."

"Because the portal was closed?" asked Pete.

"No," Roy answered, "because we pissed off the person who was profiting from the portal. In retaliation, he made them visible."

"You're right," Sarah said, taking a sip of her coffee, "I find it hard to believe. But keep going." She tapped Steven on his arm to get his attention, then pointed to the basket of muffins. Steven passed it to her.

"It costs him every time he makes them visible. I believe he'll get tired of doing it and will eventually stop," Roy said. "Also, with the portal closed, many of the ghosts that are here — the ones that came here from somewhere else, not the ones that were generated here — will go back home. That will reduce the ghost population significantly."

"But," Steven said, "that may take some time."

"How long?" Sarah asked.

"Don't know," Roy said. "Could happen quickly."

"Or," Steven added, "it might take a long time."

"Is there anything we can do?" Pete asked.

"Well, you can wait," said Roy.

"Or," said Steven, "Roy and I can hunt down the guy who's doing it, and try to convince him to stop."

No one said anything for a while. They all picked at their muffins.

"Look," Sarah said. "I've been less than friendly to you, and for that I apologize. Pete told me after you left here you went to New Mexico on our behalf. That's really kind of you. I don't know what you were doing down there, but I suspect you felt it was the right thing to do to help us."

She poured herself more coffee while she spoke.

"I don't think we'll survive more nights like last night. Pete says the deaths will stop. All right, I'll take that at face value. But if our guests are literally scared out of their rooms and into their cars, like last night, we won't survive. We'll be bankrupt in a month."

Again there was silence. Sarah sighed.

"Listen, I know I've been less than charitable. I walked into the kitchen last night when I heard gunshots. There was a dead woman on the counter and a man above her, literally sawing through her arm. He'd already cut off her other arm; it was lying on the floor. I screamed and ran out of the room and into my bedroom, and I called Pete. He told me it was happening all over the hotel and to lock myself in my room and not come out."

She popped a piece of muffin in her mouth. "When I got up this morning, Pete told me you said they'd all be gone at sunrise. Sure enough, they were. I walked into the kitchen, no sign of the woman or the man. I can't explain it, but apparently you were right — about there being a lot of ghosts here, about them disappearing in the morning, all of that. I stand corrected."

There was another long pause. No one moved or said anything.

"So," she continued, "if there's anything – *anything* – you can do that would help us, I would be extremely grateful. I have no idea what that might be, how much danger it places you in. But I think you're the only chance we've got here. You can stay as long as you need to. We'll cover your expenses. We're desperate, Mr. Hall."

She looked down at her muffin and picked another piece.

"I'm begging you," she said, looking back up at Roy.

Steven looked at Roy, and he could see him melt.

◊

Steven was behind the wheel, Roy in the passenger seat. They were in their car driving back to Seattle.

"You're doing the right thing," Steven said. "You and I might be equipped to deal with those manifestations, but they are not."

"You're probably right about that," Roy said. "Still, I wish they'd just let it sit and play out. A couple of months and it'd be fine."

"They don't have a couple of months," Roy said.

"You don't exactly understand what we're going to have to do, who this guy is," Roy said. "You think that because it's been relatively easy so far to work with Robert and Albert that we'll be just as successful with Jurgen. We won't. He's a vile little man and he's resourceful. And he's pissed. How much energy do you think it takes to make two hundred ghosts visible for a night? When he finds out we're the ones behind the shutdown of his portal, he'll direct all that energy at us."

"He's a man, right?" Steven asked. "He's not some supernatural half man, half monster?"

"As far as I know," replied Roy.

"Then he can be reasoned with," said Steven.

"You may find that harder to do than you think," Roy said.

"Why?" Steven asked.

"He has a way of getting under your skin," Roy said. "Throws you off your game. That's why I want to see Dixon before we talk to him."

"He was the friend who recognized Albert's pattern?" Steven asked.

"Yes," Roy replied. "He and I have some experience with Jurgen. Jurgen tried to take advantage of us."

Steven slowed the car down as he crossed the bridge from Oregon into Washington. It was a long bridge, spanning the Columbia river.

"What exactly happened between you two and Jurgen?" Steven asked. "He tried to rip you off?"

"Yes," Roy replied, "and then he got pissed when we called him on it!"

"Tell me the story," Steven said.

"I needed an unusual mineral," Roy explained. "I found Jurgen as a source, but he had a minimum order amount and it was far more than I needed. So I approached Dixon about going in with me on the order, if he wanted any. He said yes, so we pooled our payment to him and ordered the mineral.

"Jurgen takes our money, then tells us we owe him twice as much. He claims the minimum was per person, not per order. Dixon and I, we begin to realize we're dealing with a shady character. So we ask him to cancel the order and return our money. He won't, he says the cancel fee is equal to what we've already paid."

"Ooo," Steven said, "that *is* irritating."

"So we went back to him and said, look, we ordered as a partnership. That's a single legal entity. We also threatened to turn him in to the Secretary of State and the state Attorney General. That seemed to work; he doesn't like getting involved with any officials. He said, 'Look, because you didn't understand the rules, I'll give you the order this time,' something like that, and we both didn't care, we just wanted our money back or the mineral we'd ordered.

"So, we get the mineral, and it wasn't the right thing at all – it was completely different than what we ordered. We took it back to him and we went around and around, with him defending himself and us telling him whoever provided our order screwed up. He finally agreed to supply us with the right mineral.

"So, at this point we're pretty sick of this guy."

"I can imagine," Steven interjected.

"But that's not the end of it," Roy said. "Then we start hearing that he's bad mouthing us to other vendors, claiming we were bad customers, we ripped him off, he did us favors and we took advantage of him, that kind of thing. I doubt most people believed any of what he said because most people knew what a lowlife he was. But Dixon and I were pissed about it. First he tries to screw us every way he can, then after the deal he keeps screwing us! We didn't want people thinking we couldn't be relied upon. So we decided to stand up to him, to shut him up."

"Really?" Steven asked. "What did you do?"

"Dixon and I went to his warehouse, walked into his office, shut the door, and sat down. Then we told him if he said another word about us to anyone, we'd make it our personal mission to destroy his business. We told him we'd dig until we found every supplier he had and fuck with them. We'd track his customers and torment them. And we told him we wouldn't stop until we'd caused him enough damage to equal a thousand times what our little mineral transaction cost.

"He weaseled and hummed and hawed. He called us every name in the book. But eventually he backed off. He knew we'd do it, and it wasn't worth it to him to start some kind of war with us. There was no upside for him and a lot of negatives. We told him we'd never order from him again and to never contact us, either.

"Now it appears we're going to confront him again. That's why I want to talk to Dixon. This will involve him since he was with me when we had the run in with Jurgen years ago."

Steven realized there was more to this confrontation than he originally anticipated. He had stood up to Roy on this issue but he reminded himself that Roy was far more experienced than he was, and he needed to take that into consideration.

"We'll be getting home around nine," Steven said. "I presume our visit with Dixon will be tomorrow?"

"No, we can visit him tonight," Roy said. "He stays up all night. I think he sleeps in the middle of the day."

"Dixon is human, right?"

"Oh yes," Roy said. "Completely human. Just odd."

Thirteen

They drove through the city and into the suburb of Ballard until they reached the docks. Here a mixture of small personal boats were moored with larger commercial vessels. As they walked to the pier, Steven noticed large yachts kept under covered slips, looking very expensive. *I wonder if they ever take them out,* Steven thought, *or if they're just here as trophies.*

An occasional overhead light allowed them to keep their footing on the floating metal walkways that the boats were moored to. He could smell the saltwater. Seagulls cawed and bickered nearby. He noticed lights on in many of the smaller boats.

"Do people live in these?" he asked Roy. "Permanently?"

"Dixon does," Roy said. "His boat is his home. When he gets tired of Seattle he takes it somewhere else until he wants to come back."

After snaking through several turns, Roy led Steven down a dark floating gangway and they approached Dixon's boat. Roy stepped on board and knocked on the door.

No one answered. He knocked again. Still no reply.

"This is odd," Roy said. "Can I use your phone?"

Steven handed his phone to Roy. Roy dialed and placed it to his ear. They both heard it ringing from inside the cabin.

"Dixon, is that you?" Roy said into the phone. "We're outside, let us in."

They heard a rustling inside the boat and after a few moments a face appeared at the window in the door. The man was short, had a short grey beard that encircled the lower half of his face, and was bald on top. His eyes went wide when he saw Roy, and he smiled. Then he opened the door a little.

"I didn't think you were coming tonight!" Dixon said through the crack in the door. Steven could smell the booze on his breath.

"I knew you'd be up," Roy said. "Let us in!"

"I can't," Dixon said. Steven noticed that Dixon didn't have a shirt on. "I'm...entertaining, if you get my drift."

Roy frowned at him as though he did not know. Then he raised his eyebrows and smiled.

"You old dog," Roy said. "Who is she? This is Steven by the way."

"Hi Steven!" Dixon said, sticking his arm through the crack in the door to shake Steven's hand.

They all heard giggling from inside the boat.

"What?" Roy said. "How many have you got in there?"

"Three," Dixon said, smiling. "Capitol Hill girls. All drunk. They're suckers for houseboats."

Roy was impressed. "You have got to let me in on your secret, Dixon."

"I will, I will," he replied. "But tomorrow, OK? I need to get back to the party. How about I come over to your place? What time?"

"Make it nine," Roy said, turning to leave. "No, ten. And bring some doughnuts, it's the least you can do for me driving all the way out here."

"I will," Dixon said. "'Night, boys."

Steven and Roy turned and walked back the way they came. They heard Dixon shutting the door behind them.

"I don't understand how he does it," Roy said. "He's nearly my age, but the girls flock to him like he was forty years younger."

"Maybe he's not as crabby and cantankerous as you," Steven said. "Girls don't like crabby."

"I think he tilts things in his favor," Roy said, "with a little enhanced charm, if you know what I mean."

◊

When Steven arrived at Roy's house the next morning, Dixon was already there. It looked like Roy and Dixon had gone through half the doughnuts.

"Steven!" Roy said as he walked in. "Come on in! We were just catching up. Dixon, I introduced you last night, but this is my son Steven. You can see him proper now."

Dixon stood up from the kitchen chair he had been seated in and shook Steven's hand again. "Pleased to meet you, Steven!" he said, smiling broadly. He was thin and short and seemed energetic. *He has good cause to be,* Steven thought.

"Steven," Roy said, pulling a chair out from the table for him to join them, "grab a doughnut and we'll get started."

Dixon watched him sit, then sat in his own chair.

"Well," started Roy, "I told you on the phone, it's Jurgen again. A whole different business this time. But you know him better than me, and I thought it'd be smart to talk to you before we try to deal with him."

Dixon stirred his coffee with a spoon, never touching the sides of the cup. Then he pulled the spoon out, licked it, and placed it next to the cup. He took a sip. "Why don't you start at the beginning?" Dixon said. "I'd like to know the whole story, so I know why we've got to deal with this asshole again."

Roy began the tale, starting with their trip to Pete and Sarah in Oregon, all the way through to their last breakfast with them yesterday morning. Roy turned to Steven. "Did you hear from Pete today?" he asked him. "Was it just as bad last night?"

"Yes, he called me around seven this morning," Steven replied. "He said it was the same as the night before. He didn't sound as stressed – I think he knew what to expect, that made it easier to handle. But I'm sure they won't be able to put up guests until it stops."

"Based on what you've told me," Dixon said, "Jurgen is bound to give up after a while. He's an asshole but he's pragmatic." He picked up his spoon again and stirred his coffee in the same manner, replacing the spoon exactly the same way.

Steven looked at Roy. He knew Roy read his facial expression, which said: I expect support on this.

"Well," said Roy, "I had considered that. The problem is Pete and Sarah. They can't ride it out. It'll destroy them financially. And," he hesitated, "I'm afraid I sort of over-promised and under-delivered on this one. I told them it'd be over when we shut down the portal."

"Counting your chickens before they hatched!" said Dixon. "That's a bad habit, Roy."

"I know," Roy said, "so I sort of owe it to them to figure this out. If we can get Jurgen to stop tormenting them, that's my goal."

"He might direct that anger at us," Dixon said. "He's petty, he'd do it just to get back at us for the incident we had with him years ago."

"I know," Roy said. "That's why I wanted your advice on this. What do you think we should do?"

Dixon thought. "I don't know. I really don't."

"Where is he, exactly?" Steven asked. "You said he had a warehouse. Is it here in Seattle?"

"Yes," Roy replied, "down by the Duwamish in the industrial district. It's a front where they transfer food from one container into another and resell it. His real operation is hidden and spread out all over the West Coast."

"Is he at that warehouse?" asked Steven. "Are his offices there? Can we go meet him there?"

"I suppose so," said Roy. "That's where we dealt with him before."

"Then I propose we do that," said Steven. "We go down there, ask to see him. Tell him why we shut down the portal, find out what he wants to stop the attacks on the manor. If he's as pragmatic as you say, he'll want something out of it."

Roy turned to Dixon. "See, he doesn't realize who he's dealing with."

"You keep saying that, Dad," Steven said, "but I don't see what the big deal is. He's going to find out sooner or later. Better to have it play out on our terms."

"He's got a point, Roy," Dixon said, raising his cup to take another sip of coffee. "For this to go anywhere, we need to know what it's going to take to get him to stop. Going in forcefully might work; it worked for us before. Jurgen seems to respect that." He set his cup down in the same place, and arranged the handle to point in the same direction it had been before he picked it up. "Then again," he added, "it might get us killed."

"Do we go in with protection?" Roy asked.

"He'll take that as a threat," Dixon said. "But he'll know we're serious."

"By protection," Steven asked, "do you mean the potion, or guns?"

"Both!" Roy and Dixon answered simultaneously.

"OK," Steven replied. "Let's do it then. When do we leave?"

Roy and Dixon looked at each other. "You ready?" Roy asked him.

"Sure," Dixon said, stirring his coffee again.

"Steven," Roy said, "just remember to stay focused on what we're trying to do. He has a way of confusing people, twisting them to what he wants. If you get off your game he'll use that against you."

"I'm ready," Steven said.

◊

Steven drove them to the warehouse. It was about fifteen minutes from Roy's. Dixon sat in the back seat behind Roy. He kept raising and lowering the window.

"Dixon," Steven said, "are you hot? Should I turn on the air?"

"It won't matter," Roy said. "He'll keep doing it."

"Really?" Steven asked. "The whole way there?"

"Yes, the whole way," Roy replied.

Steven followed Roy's directions and pulled his car into a parking space next to a cement structure with no sign. White paint peeled from the walls and the windows, which had been painted over.

Roy passed around a thermos. Inside was a clear mixture that tasted like vodka. Each of the men took a couple of gulps and handed the thermos back to Roy, who capped it and placed it on the floor of the car. Steven had tasted this mixture before, when he and Roy had confronted the creatures that were haunting his house. At first Steven didn't want to have anything to do with Roy's concoction, but after he tried it, he was hooked.

They walked to the door and opened it. Inside was a large open space. There were a dozen people seated at small tables. Plastic bottles of all sizes were stacked in racks against the walls. All of the workers appeared to be Asian women; they had their hair pulled back into nets and many of them were wearing white face masks over their nose and mouth.

Roy pointed to several built-out offices in the back of the room. They walked through the work area. None of the Asian women turned or noticed them. Steven saw one of them pour liquid from a large bottle into a smaller one, cap it, and affix a label. Then she placed the small bottle into a cardboard crate on the floor.

As they walked to the offices in the back Steven felt the potion spread throughout his body, creating a sense of euphoria. He remembered what Roy had told him when he'd first tasted it, months ago: *You're not stronger, so don't get cocky. You're just protected from a mental attack.*

When they reached the offices in the back, Roy knocked on the door.

"What?" came from inside.

Roy turned to look at Steven and Dixon, then he opened the door and they all walked in.

The room was unlike any kind of managerial office Steven had ever seen. There were mounted animal heads on the walls and piles of skins on tables. There were multi-colored lights in the overhead fixtures and in lamps. There were a couple of red leather sofas. What surprised Steven the most were the velvet paintings on the walls, lit by black lights. One in particular stood out; it was surrounded by an ornate gold frame and was raised to be the most prominent item in the room. Steven stared at it. It was a painting of a tall, muscular, naked man, partially obscured on the bottom half by two women and a tiger. One of the women was making love to the tiger.

"I see you like my portrait," came the high-pitched voice of a much smaller man seated behind a desk at the far end of the room. He stood and walked over to where Steven was standing, gazing at the painting. He was an inch shorter than Steven, but heavier. His clothing was all dark; his shoes looked very expensive. He had a mustache and a constant sneer on his upper lip. The first half of a double chin could be detected under his face. He had jet black hair, which was cut short and perfect. He walked slowly and deliberately. Dixon and Roy stood a few feet away, not saying anything, waiting to see what Jurgen was up to.

"I think the artist captured my true essence," Jurgen said to Steven with a slight German accent. "That's why I had him killed just after he finished it, so he could never make anything more magnificent. I was thinking he should have shown my cock, but I suppose that would be too much for some people."

Steven looked at him. "I think it's over the top," he said. He saw Jurgen's black eyes flash. He had the same feeling he'd had when meeting Albert – that this guy was much older than he appeared.

"Well," Jurgen said, "there you go. There's no accounting for your taste if you came here with these two pricks." Jurgen turned from Steven and walked back to his desk, then he turned to Roy and Dixon. "I thought you two hacks were never going to darken my door again, remember?"

"Yes," Roy said. "I remember. We're here on another matter."

"Of course you are," Jurgen said. "You are truly gifted when it comes to stating the obvious." He turned to Steven. "Your father is a moron, you know that, don't you?" He sat in his chair behind his desk and put his feet up on it. "What do you three stooges want?"

Steven felt anger rising. The fact that Jurgen had detected Steven and Roy's familiar relationship without an introduction did not deter him. He stepped forward. "We put a stop to your harvesting of blood and ghost matter. In Oregon. Now we want you to stop the attacks there."

Jurgen took his feet off his desk and looked at Steven. "You did that?"

"Me and Roy, yes."

"How?"

"Never mind how we did it," Steven said, "we want you to stop what you're doing to the manor."

"Fuck what you want," Jurgen said, walking around his desk to approach Steven again. "Do you know how much you've cost me? Tell me how you did it, or take your old man and get out."

"We talked with the contractor of the portal," Roy said calmly. "He shut it down."

"And who was that?" Jurgen asked, still staring at Steven.

Dixon broke from Roy and started walking around the back end of the room.

"A man named Robert Maysill," Roy said. "You didn't bother to find out how that tunnel was opening? You just took advantage of it without knowing anything about it? Typical."

Jurgen noticed Dixon moving laterally. They were surrounding him.

"There's no chance Maysill will reopen it," Roy said. "Not with you there taking advantage of it."

"And now you're here," Jurgen snarled at Roy, "upset that that poor man and his pregnant cunt have to put up with a few spooks in their house."

"We want you to stop," Steven said angrily. "With the portal closed, the ghosts are going to dissipate anyway. You're wasting your time cursing it every night."

"Do you ever play poker with this boy?" Jurgen asked Roy. "I imagine you'd win a lot of hand jobs from him."

Dixon began chanting quietly. Jurgen walked to his desk and opened a small wooden box. Then he walked back to Roy and Steven. After a moment Dixon became silent.

Steven knew something had happened, but he didn't know what. He decided to drop into the flow to see if he could detect what Jurgen had done.

Sitting on Dixon's head was an insect that looked like a dragonfly, but it was two or three times as large. Its tail was curved down towards Dixon's temple, and a large stinger was positioned an inch from his skin. Dixon knew something was on him. He was standing very still. Steven exited the flow.

"Don't move, Dixon," Steven said. "It's some kind of insect. On your head. With a stinger."

"Found it in Brazil," Jurgen said. "An outfit there trains them. It's waiting for a command. You can probably guess what happens if I give it."

Dixon looked petrified. He was holding his body as still as a corpse.

"Look," Roy said, "I realize you lost some revenue when the portal shut down. We're here to find out what it's going to take for you to stop the attacks."

"What, no strong arm tactics like before? I'm disappointed. You two were so determined and forceful years ago, coming in here and threatening me like I was a little girl you wanted to fuck. You don't want to fuck me again? You want to talk now? To negotiate?"

"Just tell us what you want to drop the attacks," Steven said.

"Tell your idiot spawn to shut up," Jurgen said to Roy. "Tell him, or Dixon's going to have a terrible headache."

"Steven," Roy said calmly, "let me handle this."

"Yes!" Jurgen said, turning to Steven. "Shut up and let your doddering old fuck of a father talk for you. You negotiate like a five year old. I'll bet your balls are the size of raisins, right? Am I right?"

Steven pressed his lips together to avoid saying anything. His anger was boiling inside him. Roy had been right about Jurgen's ability to get under your skin.

"Not so much to say now?" Jurgen said. "You've raised pathetic children, Roy. Tiny balls, tiny brains. Sputtering with contempt and anger like water popping out of a frying pan."

"Listen," Roy said, staying focused, "the portal isn't going to reopen unless you can afford to pay for it. It'd probably cost you more to reopen it than you've made in profit off it. If you did, we'd fight you due to our obligation to the people there. So the portal is done."

"And my supply of blood?" Jurgen said, raising his voice. "Do you know how much I get for pregnant blood? It may not pay for a portal, but it's more than you can afford."

"I wonder what people would think if they knew you traded that kind of blood," Roy said. "Many wouldn't do business with you anymore."

"And many more would!" Jurgen said. "Don't threaten me, you old fuck. What do you know about business? You run around with your imbecile son claiming to help people when all you really do is make it worse. You don't know anything about my business, you can't even handle your own correctly. Try another angle."

"A trade," Roy said. "We'll give you something in exchange for you doing as we ask."

Jurgen paused. He seemed interested in this. "What could you possibly trade that would have value to me?"

"I don't know," Roy said. "What you value is foreign to me. Tell me what you want and maybe I can match it."

Jurgen walked back to his desk and sat in his chair. "I can't think of anything. Unless..."

"Yes?" Roy asked.

"Well," Jurgen said, "there is one thing. I doubt you could do it, though, if you take along that child."

"What is it?" Roy asked.

Jurgen paused. "There is a grave I want marked."

Roy didn't alter his facial expression. "Go on," he said.

"You mark it, I'll stop cursing that house in Oregon."

"Whose grave?" asked Roy.

"That's the deal, take it or leave it," Jurgen said. "Just say yes or no."

Roy looked at Steven. Steven nodded.

"I'll do it," Roy said. Jurgen stood up and walked to the wooden box on the table. He shut the lid.

"You can relax, Dixon," Jurgen said. "Your partner here has made a deal."

He turned and walked to a cabinet behind his desk. He pulled out several small drawers until he found what he was looking for. It was in a small cloth bag. Then he sat at his desk, took a piece of note paper, and began writing on it.

"These are coordinates," Jurgen said. "The grave is somewhere near this location. It's not precise, but it's close. You'll have to search."

He handed the paper and the bag to Roy. "All you have to do is locate the precise spot of the grave. It won't be marked with a headstone. Pour the contents on the ground over the grave. Then you're done."

He turned and walked back behind his desk. "The moment you do this, I'll stop the attacks in Oregon."

"How do we know you'll keep your end of the bargain?" Steven said.

"You'll just have to trust me!" Jurgen said. "I don't suppose you noticed how your father did that, while you were playing with your dick. Cut a real man's deal. Too busy pissing on yourself like a baby, giving yourself away."

"We're going," Roy said. "Do we contact you when it's done?"

"No," Jurgen replied. "My people will smell it as soon as you pour it. *Do not* open it until you're ready to mark the grave, or you'll have some visitors you don't want. Just pour it and leave."

"What if there's more than one grave near these coordinates?" Roy asked. "How will we know which one you want marked?"

"Oh, you'll know when you find it," Jurgen said. "It'll be off the scale."

"Why us?" Steven asked. "Why don't you do it yourself?"

"Because," Jurgen said, "I can't get within fifty miles of it. I've been barred from the whole area. I ran afoul of the locals. Inbred redskin whores, the lot."

"We'll expect you to keep your side of this arrangement," Roy said. "We'll go do this, but you had better come through." Roy turned to walk out of the office.

Jurgen just laughed as they left.

Fourteen

Back at Roy's place, the three discussed the meeting with Jurgen.

"You're right," said Steven, "he's an obnoxious little fucker. I can't think of anyone I've met in my life that I dislike more."

"You played into him," Roy said "He does that so you'll get angry and give up what you really want."

"Which is what I did," Steven said, "when I told him we wanted him to stop the attacks."

"Yes," said Dixon. "He knew the value of his bargaining chip at that point."

"Sorry guys," Steven said, "but he really pissed me off."

"He pissed us off too," Dixon said, "but you notice how your father handled it. Cool as a cucumber."

"Yes, I gotta hand it to you, Dad," Steven said, "you handled him pretty well. And you got him to agree to a deal."

"Well," Roy said, "I've dealt with him before. Made it easier not to get sidetracked with his insults."

"What I think you two need to worry about," Dixon said, "is why he's interested in that grave. You might be creating another mess."

"If it has anything to do with Jurgen," Roy said, "it's one of two possibilities. Either the contents of the grave are extremely valuable and he wants them to sell, or the contents of the grave will harm us or kill us, which would be his way of getting back at us for shutting down the portal."

"Or both," Dixon said. "His desire for retribution is only exceeded by his desire for profit, so it's more likely the contents are valuable rather than dangerous. But with him, who knows."

"What do you think we should do?" Roy asked Dixon.

"I think you should go check it out," Dixon said. "But first find out who put the barrier in place. That'll give you some idea why Jurgen wants to know the location of that grave. I'll help you out with that, but the rest of this thing is up to you two to do. I'm not getting more involved than that."

"I understand," Roy said. "And you've been a good sport to go along with us this far. And I'm sorry about that thing on your head."

Dixon frowned and swatted at the air above his head.

"No, not now," Roy said. "Back at Jurgen's."

"Oh," Dixon said.

"Will the barrier Jurgen talked about have a signature, like the tunnel?" asked Steven.

"Yes," said Dixon. "And I'm a bit of an expert in patterns. You find out what the pattern is, call me, and I'll get you pointed in the right direction."

"Thanks for that," said Roy.

"Will you use a mirror again, like the tunnel?" Steven asked Roy.

"A mirror should work, right Dixon?" asked Roy.

"Mirrors work fine, unless the barrier is unusual," Dixon replied.

"First we will have to locate the barrier itself," said Roy. "It stops Jurgen, but it won't stop us. We won't feel it. In order to detect it, we'll have to get very high."

Steven paused. At first he thought his dad was saying they'd need to toke on some weed. He smiled at the thought.

"I'm not joking," Roy said. "If it's fifty miles wide, we're going to have to go pretty high to spot it."

Dixon chuckled. "Use arganthumum. Sixteen p try janth and gors to yavlen," he said to Roy.

"What?" asked Steven. "Is that Swedish?"

Both Roy and Dixon laughed. "No," Roy said. "It's English. You just don't understand it."

"Oh," Steven said, "like the book."

"Yes," said Roy, "like the book."

"Don't worry," Dixon said, rising and slapping Steven on the back. "You'll keep picking it up. Listen to your old man, he knows what he's doing." He started to walk towards the door. "I'm headed home guys."

"Thanks for your advice and help," Roy said. "I'll give you a call when we get the pattern from that barrier."

"I do want to hear all about it when it's done," Dixon said. "I'll take you both out for a sail on my boat, and we'll tell stories."

"That sounds like a plan," Roy said. Steven walked Dixon to the door, shook his hand as he left. Dixon stepped between the inside and the outside of the door frame twice, then walked to his car. Steven walked back in to Roy.

"Would you figure out where these coordinates are?" Roy asked, handing Steven the paper Jurgen had given him.

Steven took the paper and looked at the numbers. *I even hate his handwriting,* Steven thought. He punched the numbers into Google on his phone.

"Northern California," he said. "Middle of nowhere, about two hours northwest of Sacramento."

"Want to drive it?" Roy asked.

"Sure," Steven said. "Give me an hour to go home and get new clothes, and I'll come back and pick you up."

◊

As they drove south on I-5 towards the Oregon border, Steven thought about the mistakes he'd made at Jurgen's place earlier in the day. Roy had warned him about Jurgen, but he'd let the guy get to him anyway. He had become particularly angry when Jurgen attacked Roy and Pete and Sarah. *He didn't attack them,* Steven thought. *He just spoke words. He called them names.* To Roy it was water off a duck's back, but Steven had let it get to him, let it inflame him. *I fucked up,* he thought. *Roy warned me, and I let him get to me anyway. I'm going to have to work on that.*

He sighed. Roy heard him.

"Don't kick yourself over it," Roy said, aware of what was bothering him. "We survived it. We're fine."

"You don't realize how angry he made me," Steven said.

"Oh, I do," Roy replied. "I was just as angry."

"But you didn't let it show," Steven said.

"Didn't I? Well, I'm glad to hear that!"

"That's my point," Steven said. "We were both angry. But you didn't let it show. Jurgen used that against me, against us. I worry that I'm a liability to you."

"Oh, shut up," Roy said. "You're not a liability."

"I worry I'll let myself react the same way in some future situation. It could cost us more, or be dangerous to us both."

"You won't," said Roy, "because you'll learn from this. You aren't a liability, son. You're an asset. That's how I feel about it, anyway."

Steven drove the car on in silence. He resolved to take the warnings his father gave him more seriously and to gain some control over his anger. They were battling evil characters that would take advantage of you as soon as look at you. They needed every leg up they could get to survive it; they didn't need to shoot themselves in the feet.

He pressed the accelerator and picked up speed. Soon they'd be in California, hunting for a grave. It reminded him of the hunt he'd done with Roy back in Seattle. *At least this one we don't have to dig up*, he thought.

◊

They spent the night in Grant's Pass. They considered driving on to the manor and staying with Pete and Sarah, but it would add two hours to the trip and Roy didn't want to get sidetracked. Steven suspected it was partially because they didn't have much to tell them yet and Roy wanted to avoid Pete and Sarah until he had something substantial.

Steven stopped in Medford to pick up a GPS that could be handheld, give exact coordinates, and respond to satellites, not cell towers. He bought extra batteries for it and they proceeded on their way.

They turned off I-5 many hours later and onto Highway 20. Clearlake was about an hour away. Steven let Roy drive so he could mess with the handheld GPS and figure it out.

"I've got a signal," Steven said, after he learned how to punch in the coordinates. "Do you want to go straight there?"

"Can you tell how far away it is?" Roy asked.

"Fifty miles, the direction we're heading," Steven answered.

"Well," Roy replied, "it's thirty to Clearlake. Let's head into town and get a place to stay. Our first goal is to inspect the barrier, if we can. We'll get to the grave eventually."

They drove until they entered Clearlake, resting at the southern end of the body of water it was named after. They found a motel as dusk settled on the town. Steven told the desk clerk they wanted to stay several nights, open ended.

As they were hauling their things into the motel room, Roy told Steven, "Come over when you're situated. We'll do the trance from there."

Steven unpacked his things and walked back over to Roy's room. Roy pulled a chair from under a table. It looked like the upholstery hadn't been cleaned in years. He sat in the chair, and Steven applied the blindfold.

"Give me a minute to get the trance set up," Roy said, "then jump in."

"Will do," Steven replied, turning off the lights in the room and sitting next to Roy on the bed.

Steven waited five minutes, then slipped into the River. He marveled at the ease with which he took this step; when he had first tried, it seemed a monumental effort. Now he found himself able to jump in and out without hesitation. *Like a kid jumping in the swimming pool,* he thought.

He saw Roy inside his trance, and Roy opened it to him. Then they rose above the motel and kept rising rapidly.

We're going to go very high for this, he heard Roy think. *Don't let it freak you out. Here, eat this.*

Roy handed Steven something and Steven took it. It looked like a small piece of bread. He couldn't feel it; it felt like nothing. He placed it to his mouth and took a bite of it. He couldn't taste or feel any of it. He had never eaten anything while in the flow, and he wondered if things always tasted like nothing when eaten this way.

It's a compound I got from Dixon, Steven heard Roy think. He saw Roy take a bite from a piece in his hand. *We'll need it to not pass out.*

You can pass out inside the flow? Steven thought.

Yes, Roy thought. *Something to do with radiation. What you just ate will help.*

They kept ascending; Steven felt compelled to hold his breath, but he exhaled and found he could take a breath easily.

We're not going to stay up long, he heard Roy think. *We just want to go high enough to make out the edges of the barrier. If you start to feel confused, that's a sign we need to go back down.*

As they rose, the lights from the town of Clearlake became fainter. Soon they could see the entire circumference of the lake and the tiny lights that dotted the edges of it. Steven felt a sense of exhilaration. This was not like looking out the windows of a plane. He was hanging in the air, free to move, not feeling gravity's pull. It gave him an overwhelming sense of freedom.

There, do you see it? he heard Roy think.

Steven saw a thin line, illuminated, running north and south many miles past the lake. He turned and saw that the line arced to bend west at a point not far from where they were rising. It circled around and back up north. They couldn't see where the north edge connected.

Let's drift more that direction, he heard Roy think. *We'll try to get the entire scope of it.*

They continued rising, and now they were moving away from the lake and into lands covered with forest. Once they saw the northern edge of the line, they stopped and turned 360 degrees in the air. They could see the entire ring. Some of it was faint, but they could make it out.

It's huge, Steven thought.

At least eighty miles wide, maybe more, Roy thought.

How do we detect the signature? Steven thought.

We'll need to go to one of the edges. Let's pick the one at the south end, it was closest to the lake.

They drifted southward rapidly, descending at the same time. Steven felt as though he was on the most thrilling roller coaster he'd ever ridden.

As they came closer to the ground and the edge of the barrier, Roy guided them to an area that had no houses or people. The line ran through a small clearing over the hill from a road. *I think we'll have some privacy here. Make note of this place. We'll have to find it tomorrow on foot.*

Steven rose from the spot and looked for markers, guideposts he could use when they returned. *All right*, he thought. *I've got it.*

They retreated from the flow and found themselves in Roy's motel room. Steven turned on the light while Roy removed the blindfold.

"All right, what's the plan for tomorrow?" Steven asked.

"We'll go to that clearing," Roy said. "I'll bring a mirror. We'll jump in the flow and try to get the pattern of the barrier. Then I'll call Dixon and we'll see what our next step will be."

"Do you want to turn in?" Steven asked.

"Yes," Roy answered. "I'm tired. We've been doing a hell of a lot of driving."

"I gotta say," Steven remarked, "that ride up into the clouds was remarkable."

"Yeah, that was pretty fun," Roy said. "That stuff you ate will last a while. But don't do it all night long, OK? We got work to do tomorrow."

"No, I won't," Steven said, closing the door to Roy's room. "Good night."

◊

It took them some time to locate the exact road they'd tried to memorize the night before. As they were trying to locate it, Steven took a call from Pete. Pete said the hauntings were still visible at the manor the past two nights, and Sarah was still keeping the hotel vacant. He told them he'd devised ways to walk around the most troubling ones. He'd also discovered that some were on schedules, and they were learning which times of the night to avoid certain ghosts.

Steven turned to Roy with the phone at his ear. "Pete wants to know what time you ran into Dennington, in the hallway."

"Must have been around midnight," Roy said, recalling the interaction. "Why, has he seen him?"

"He says it was around midnight, Pete," Steven said back into the phone. "Well, good luck with that. We're making progress here and we'll give you an update soon. Hang in there." Steven hung up.

"Has he seen him?" Roy asked again.

"No, but he wants to," Steven said. "He made friends with a pretty woman in the gazebo, and now he's interested in meeting the cordial ones before we turn them all off. He remembered Dennington from your description of him at breakfast that one morning. Now he wants to get to know him!"

"Well, at least it gives him something to do," Roy said.

"On the other hand," Steven said, "Sarah is still terrified. She stays locked in her room all night."

"Poor thing," Roy replied. "She should come out and enjoy herself."

They drove in silence a little ways further until Steven recognized a marker he'd noted the night before.

"That split tree, there," he said, pointing over the hill to their left. "That's it. We need to walk over that hill."

Steven pulled the car to the side of the road. The road was small and quiet; they had passed only one other car while on it. They walked over to a fence and Steven held open the barbed wire for Roy to bend under, then Roy returned the favor.

They walked over the hill until they reached the clearing.

"Yes," Roy said, "this is it. Let's move as close to it as we can get."

They positioned themselves based on their memory from the previous night. Steven slipped into the River, but was unable to see the barrier. He tried feeling for it, but nothing registered.

"Don't feel bad," Roy said. "They're hard enough to detect at night, let alone during the daylight. I'm going to have to trance to find it. You hold the mirror right there. I'll be right back."

Roy sat cross-legged on the ground and wrapped the blindfold around his eyes. Steven stood above him, holding the mirror at the angle Roy had identified. Several minutes went by. Steven became aware of how strange they must look if anyone happened to see them.

Roy emerged from the flow and stood up, removing the blindfold. "All right, I think I have it." Steven lowered the mirror. Roy took a small notepad from his shirt pocket and sketched a few lines. "Let's go!"

They walked back to the car and got in.

"Do you have any reception here?" Roy asked Steven.

Steven checked his phone. "No, no bars," he said. "Let's drive back towards town."

After several minutes of driving, Steven checked his phone again. Two bars appeared. "Here you go," he said, handing the phone to Roy. Roy dialed Dixon and they chatted. Roy described the pattern. Then there was a long wait.

"He's looking," Roy said to Steven. "He's got these patterns all drawn out, he's trying to find a match."

Dixon came back on the line, and Roy started writing down information. "Got it, yes," Roy said to Dixon on the phone. "Thank you for all your help with this Dixon. Yes. Oh, would you? Yes, we'll head there now. Yes, I'll let you know." Then he hung up.

"Her name is Eliza Winters. And she lives right in Clearlake."

"Well," Steven said, "that's convenient! At least we don't have to go to another state."

"I suspect," Roy said, handing the phone back to Steven, "living inside the barrier makes it easier for her to maintain. It'll be interesting to see what she has to say."

"Do you have an address for her?" Steven asked.

"Right here," Roy said, brandishing the notepad.

"I'd have you enter it into my phone for directions," Steven said, "but I know that's not going to happen."

"Damn right it isn't," said Roy. "That thing is for calling. Why does it have to be for anything else?"

"Show me the address," Steven said. Roy held the address up for Steven to read. Then he said to Roy, "Watch this!"

He pressed a button on his phone, and spoke into it: "Directions to 480 East Wilson Street, Clearlake, California."

"Getting directions to 480 East Wilson Street" came the reply back from the phone. Then it said, "Head north for eighteen miles, then turn right onto East Main street." Steven beamed at Roy.

"Well, I'll be goddamned!" Roy said. "Does it wipe your ass, too?"

Fifteen

Eliza's house looked like a mansion, albeit a run-down one. The exterior wood was exposed over most of the house, leaving a weather-beaten look. It stood three stories high and had beautiful bay windows masked from the inside by tightly drawn blinds.

Steven and Roy walked through the front yard. There were large, overgrown bushes that needed tending and the lawn was three weeks past its expiration date. Once they walked up onto the porch, they saw the front door was open behind a screen door. They could hear the sounds of a video game coming from beyond.

Steven knocked on the door.

"Mom!" a child yelled from inside.

They knocked again. "Mom!" came the reply.

"Hello!" Steven said through the screen. "Is anyone home?"

They heard the sounds of the game abruptly stop and a boy of about ten walked around a corner and to the door.

"Hello?" he said sheepishly.

"We're looking for Eliza Winters," Roy asked.

The boy turned and walked down a hallway out of sight. In the distance they heard him yell again, "Mom!" and then he turned and walked back into the room he came from. The explosions of the video game resumed.

A woman appeared, walking down the hallway toward the door. She was large framed. Her hair was long and wild, swirling around her head as she walked, creating a sense of chaos that Steven found disarming. As she approached the door and Steven saw her features, his alarm subsided. She had a soft countenance and her blue eyes were alive, moving rapidly, taking them in. He liked her instantly.

"You must be Roy," she said, opening the screen door. "Please come in. Forgive my son for not asking you in. I assure you he's been taught the proper way to greet guests but he chooses to forget, something I will remind him about after you leave. And you are?"

"This is my son Steven," Roy said.

She extended her hand. "Eliza Winters, how nice to meet you." Her voice had a lilt and charm that Steven found mesmerizing. He felt he could listen to it forever.

"Nice to meet you too," he said back to her.

"Please, have a seat, I'll be right back," she said, and turned to leave the room. They could overhear her speaking with the boy and the sound from the video game diminished by half. She came back a few minutes later with a pitcher of iced tea and three glasses.

"I just made this when Dixon called," she said, pouring them each a glass, "so it's fresh. Nothing worse than old tea. Dixon is such a cute old man, I just think the world of him."

Steven thought of the girls on the boat in Ballard, and wondered if Eliza had slept with Dixon.

"No, I haven't slept with him," she said, "though I might if the opportunity presented itself. He is so charming, the little rascal."

Steven looked away from her, embarrassed. *Can she read my thoughts?* he wondered.

"I can't read all thoughts, Steven," she said, "just the strong ones. And since men think about sex on average once every seven seconds, you were easy. I'll bet you take sugar with your tea," she said, scooping some sugar with a long spoon and handing the glass to Steven.

"Yes, I do," Steven said, taking the glass, "And I thought that was a myth. The seven seconds thing."

"Not in my experience. And you Roy? No sugar for you, am I right?"

"You are indeed!" Roy said. He seemed as delighted with her as Steven.

"Well then," she said, taking a glass for herself and leaning back in her chair, "I hope this hits the spot for you. Trancing around in fields probably worked up a thirst."

"Dixon told you?" Roy asked.

"No, I saw it," she said. "As soon as you tranced right next to it, alarms went off here. That's a cute little blindfold you use!" she said, smiling and pointing at him. Roy blushed.

"Well," Steven said, "I hope you don't think we were trying to mess with it in any way."

"Oh no," she said. "Until Dixon called I was concerned, but he wouldn't have sent you to me if you weren't good people. Why don't you tell me why you were trying to find me?"

Roy took another sip of the tea and sat his glass down. "Well," he said, "we were hoping to find out why you have the barrier in the first place."

"There are several reasons for the barrier," she replied. "Some of it I can talk about, and some of it I can't. Maybe if you could tell me why you're interested, I could decide how much I can tell."

"Fair enough," Roy said. "Do you know Jurgen?"

She nodded.

"It's a long story as to why, but he wants us to mark a grave not far from here."

She leaned forward in her chair. "Does he? That little bugger!"

"Yes," Steven jumped in, "and we thought we'd find out more about why he's barred from the area before we proceed."

"You haven't marked it yet?" she asked.

"No," said Roy. "I don't trust Jurgen farther than I can throw him. We told him we'd do it to get him to stop tormenting some people we're trying to help. But before we actually do it, I want to know why he wants it."

Eliza eyed them both for a minute before she spoke.

"OK," she said, "I'm gonna tell you. Because Dixon vouched for you, and I believe your story. But this cannot go past this room, and I want a blood oath from both of you before I do."

"OK," Roy said.

"Yours or mine?" she asked.

"Yours," Roy said. "I didn't bring one."

Eliza stood and walked to the mantle of the fireplace. There was a small box made of marble. She opened it and withdrew a knife. She handed it to Roy.

Roy took the blade and ran it against the palm of his left hand. Then he raised his hand and looked at Eliza. "I swear an elemental oath that the information you share with me I will not share with anyone, except Steven here, without your consent."

He handed the knife to Steven. "Do the same thing," he instructed.

"Uh," Steven said, unsure if he wanted to proceed. He looked up at Roy, and then at Eliza.

"Never taken an elemental oath before?" she asked.

"He's new," Roy said. "In training."

"I see," she said. "Well, Steven, are you going to keep what I share with you private?"

"Yes," he said.

"Then take the oath. As your father did."

"I'm not sure that I know what it means," Steven said. "And I'd like to know what I'm agreeing to."

"That's smart," she said. "You are wise to ask. It means that I will have confidence that you will honor the oath. Because if you do not, you will have already given us permission to turn your blood to fire and your flesh to stone. That's allegory of course; you're basically giving us permission to kill you if you break the oath. So be sure."

"I will not tell anyone," he said, holding the knife.

"Then what are you waiting for?" she asked.

He looked at the knife, expecting to see Roy's blood, but none was there.

"It's a special knife," Eliza said. "It consecrates the oath."

Steven ran the blade against his left palm. It stung, and blood began to drip from his hand. He spoke the same words he had heard Roy say, then lowered his hand. Once he was done, the sting was gone. He looked at his hand and there was no cut. He rubbed the spot with his right hand to be sure.

Eliza held out her hand for the knife. Steven handed it back to her. She returned it to the box on the mantle.

"You'll want to be sure your boy doesn't get into that box," Steven said with a laugh.

"It doesn't open for him," she said, returning to her seat.

Steven adjusted uncomfortably in his seat.

"I told you there are multiple reasons for the barrier," she began. "That's true. The first reason is to keep scavengers like Jurgen out. Whenever we run across someone of his kind, we add them to the barred list. There's eight or nine people barred. Several species of creatures, too. We don't want them anywhere around here so we just keep them out altogether.

"But we can't keep out everyone. So the second reason for the barrier is a demarcation. The entire area inside the barrier is protected."

"Oh?" Roy said. "Protected how?"

"Artifacts move. When someone digs for one, it moves down in the earth. Slips away from them before they can reach it. You and I would know they're moving, but the average person digging in the ground never sees anything. That's how we keep them buried and in this area."

"Is there a third reason?" Steven asked.

"That's the most serious reason, and it's the reason for the oath. We have a demon buried here."

Roy didn't say anything. It clicked for Steven.

"That's what he's after. Wow, Jurgen is really an asshole!" Steven said. "Excuse my French."

"Do you know where it's buried?" Roy asked.

"If I did, I couldn't tell you," she said. "That's tightly guarded."

"Do you think Jurgen knows where it's buried?" Roy asked Eliza.

"I would find that hard to believe," she replied. "In four hundred years only a handful of people know the exact location."

"That's how long it's been buried?" Steven asked.

"Yes," she said, "and we take our responsibility to keep it buried seriously. That demon was one of the worst to ever walk the earth. Even its remains in the ground pollute things around here. That's one of the reasons we don't like artifacts being dug up."

"I'm guessing he would be able to sell it for a lot of money?" Steven asked.

"I would think he'd grind it up," Roy said. "I imagine as an ingredient he make far more off it."

"A spoonful would be worth millions to certain people," Eliza said. "It would also cause immense misery. We'll never let it be dug up. It's staying in the ground."

"What are we going to do?" Steven asked. "We're at a dead end here. Go back to Jurgen? We took an oath, we can't tell him what we know! We've boxed ourselves in."

"I suspect," Roy said, "that even if we'd gone to that grave and tried to mark it, I would have detected something was very wrong with it."

"You wouldn't have gotten within a hundred yards of it," Eliza said. "It's heavily monitored."

"Why would Jurgen send us to mark a grave we wouldn't be able to get to?" Roy asked. "Do you think he just stumbled across coordinates and doesn't know what they are?"

"Coordinates?" Eliza asked. "He gave you specific coordinates?"

"Yes," Steven said, looking for the paper with the coordinates in his pocket. "He said the grave would be somewhere near them. Not precise, but close. He said we'd have to narrow it down on our own, then mark it." Steven handed the paper to Eliza.

"Eew," she scrunched up her nose. "Did he write this?"

"Yes," said Roy.

"It stinks!" she said, looking it over.

"Funny," Steven said, "I didn't notice a smell."

"I'm sensitive to bad odors," she said, holding it at arm's length. She studied it for a second, then handed it back.

"That's not it," she said, taking a drink of iced tea.

"Not it?" Steven asked. "Not the location of the demon's grave?"

"I can't say any more than that," she said. "But it's a relief."

"So he's sent us after some other grave?" Roy asked. "There has to be something special about it, he wouldn't send us to mark a normal grave in a barred area when he can find plenty in areas he *can* access."

"Unless his goal was to discover you by tracking us," Steven said, indicating Eliza.

"I'm easily discovered," Eliza said. "I'm in the directory. The signature's there for everyone to see. And the house is protected. Anything said inside cannot be detected outside."

"Perhaps he intends to press us for information, since we've visited with you," Steven said.

"What do you know?" she said. "Even if he tortures you, which he won't, you don't know the location of the demon. The most you could give up is its existence. And you won't do that, because it would mean your death."

"I don't think that was his intent," Roy said. "I don't think he knows anything about the demon here. I think there's something about that grave that interests him, and he wants it."

"And I," Eliza said, "of course, cannot allow him to dig it up if it's inside the barrier. If you mark it, we'll stop whoever he sends in to obtain it."

"If we mark it, we'll be able to call our end of the deal done, regardless," Steven said.

"No," Roy said, "I know him. If he doesn't get that body – or whatever is in that grave – he will *not* consider the deal done. He's slimy that way. He'll keep tormenting Pete and Sarah until he gets something that he feels compensates him for the closure of the portal."

"Sounds like you've been on quite an adventure, boys," Eliza said. "Here, have another glass of tea. I want to hear all about it."

Roy and Steven took turns telling the events of the past week to Eliza. She listened carefully, occasionally asking questions and getting them to clarify things. When it was over she leaned back in her chair and sighed.

"That is one hell of a story," she said. The clock on the mantle chimed once. "And look, it's an hour past lunch time. You'll both stay?"

Steven and Roy looked at each other. "If it's not an imposition," Steven offered.

"I'd be offended if you didn't," Eliza said, taking them both back into the kitchen, where she began to fix sandwiches and refilled their iced tea glasses for the third time. They chatted about the area and how long she'd had the house, if she was married (she wasn't) and how many kids she had (the one boy). When the sandwiches were ready, she went into the video game room and they heard the sounds stop.

"Mom!" the boy's voice cried from the other room.

"Lunch is ready, get your butt up off that couch and into the kitchen."

As the boy entered the room, Eliza introduced Steven and Roy. "And this is Troy," she said. "He's ten and plays far too many video games."

"Mom!" he said, sitting down at the table.

"In the time I've been here," Steven said to Troy, "I've only ever heard you say 'Mom!'" Do you say anything else?"

Troy lowered his face, embarrassed. "Yes," he said.

Steven and Roy laughed. Eliza sat a plate of sandwiches in the center of the table, and everyone reached for one.

"What grade are you in?" Roy asked Troy.

"Fourth," he replied.

"Is it the weekend?" Steven asked. "I've completely lost track of time, we've been so busy with this."

"Saturday," said Troy. "No school!"

"There will be no more video games," Eliza said, "until I see that grass cut."

"Mom!" Troy wailed, tossing his sandwich onto his plate.

"And don't show off in front of guests," she added. "I imagine they had to mow their lawn when they were boys."

"He made me do it with a push mower!" Steven said to Troy, pointing at Roy. "And we had a huge yard. Do you know how long that took me?"

"He's your Dad?" Troy asked Steven.

"Yes," Steven replied, "he is."

"I don't have a Dad," Troy said. "My Mom won't let me have one."

"You say that as though it's like getting a dog," Steven said.

"It would be," Eliza said, getting up from the table to retrieve a salt shaker from the counter. "He'd just eat a lot and I'd have to pick up his shit."

Roy and Steven half-laughed at this. Troy stuffed the last of his sandwich into his mouth and bolted out the kitchen door into the back yard.

"Seems like a good kid," Steven said.

"He is," she said. "Typical ten year old."

"Does he know about your abilities?" Roy asked.

"No," she said. "Not sure when's the right time for that. They say to wait until they're an adult, but who knows. When did you tell him?" she asked Roy, pointing at Steven.

"About a month ago," Roy said.

Eliza seemed impressed. "Well," she said, "when he said you were in training, I would have guessed a couple of years, not a month." She winked at him. Steven smiled.

They chatted for a while longer. Steven grew to like her even more. Her company was comfortable and her manner calming and reassuring. Sitting at the kitchen table she listened to Roy tell stories about Steven when he was little, and Steven tell how Roy had helped eliminate the ghosts from his house, and how he'd learned of Roy's gift. She asked them questions and kept refilling their iced tea.

"Can I use your bathroom?" Steven asked. "The iced tea has built up."

"Oh," she said, "of course. Just down the hall there, and to the left."

Steven walked down the hallway and to the bathroom. He shut the door and relieved himself. He could hear Troy yelling outside, kicking something around. The bathroom had typical feminine touches and was immaculately clean. When he was finished, he walked back into the kitchen to join Roy and Eliza.

"Eliza has invited us to stay here while we figure this out," Roy said.

"There's no need for you to stay at a motel," she said, pouring Steven another iced tea. He waved his hand no, but she poured anyway. "One more won't hurt," she said. "There's two empty rooms upstairs. There's two bathrooms up there as well, so we'll have plenty of room."

"Well," Steven said, hesitating. The idea seemed like a good one, if they weren't imposing.

"Now I insist," she said. "Roy, tell him this is where you're going to stay. I think you could both use an extra mind working on this problem you've got."

"You're right about that," Roy said.

Steven looked at Roy, and Roy didn't seem to be against the idea. "All right," he said. "We'll move our things from the motel."

"Glad to hear it!" she said. "We're having chicken pasta for dinner."

"We've been eating on the run for so long," Roy said, "a real meal will be a treat."

Sixteen

Later that night, after Steven and Roy had transferred their things, after the chicken and pasta, and after Troy had gone to bed, Eliza invited them upstairs. "There's something I want to show you," she said.

They ascended the staircase and stopped on the second floor landing. She pointed up the stairs to the third floor.

"If you go up this way, you'll find all the doors up there locked. It's completely sealed off. I tell Troy we keep it that way because I don't want to pay for heating up there or spending the time to keep it cleaned."

She led them through the second story hallway to the back room, which was a large room with dividing doors that opened into a second large room. They passed through both rooms and headed towards a small door on the back wall. There was very little furniture in either room, and a few toys were scattered around.

"Troy plays in here, but we don't use it for much else."

She opened the door in the back of the room, revealing a staircase.

"It goes down to the first floor and the basement. They could entertain in this large room and had easy access to the kitchen. We, however, are going up."

The staircase going up to the third floor was much narrower than the one going down. It was just tall enough to accommodate Steven, and he felt his claustrophobia coming on. It twisted right making several corners. When they reached the top, Eliza opened a door and they all walked into a large room similar in size and shape to the one they had just left.

"Troy thinks this door is locked liked the others," she said, closing the door after they'd entered. "He's never been up here."

Here was the lair Steven had been hoping to see at Albert's in Santa Fe. The walls were lined with bookcases crammed with books. There were several work tables filled with projects and plastic and glass containers filled with various objects. A large oversized chair and a couch draped with tapestries formed a small sitting area next to the work tables. It looked comfortable, inviting, and immensely interesting.

"Very impressive," Roy said. "If my wife hadn't forced me to keep my gift quiet, I might have had a room like this."

"Well, Roy," Eliza said, "you could start one now if you like. Unless you want to keep honoring that promise to her."

"No," Roy said, "I broke the promise when I showed Steven. The promise ended when she passed on."

"What I really wanted you to see," she said, walking over to one of the tables, "was this."

She lifted up a silver dome that looked like a food cloche. Underneath was another dome, made of light.

"This is what you saw this morning in the clearing, right about there," she said, pointing to a spot on the ground under the dome.

Steven moved in for a closer look. The entire geography of the area was represented under the dome of light. He could see the exact boundaries of the barrier, more precisely illustrated than what he and Roy had seen while in the flow the night before. As he watched he could see tiny lights moving on the ground.

"This is how you knew about our trance yesterday?" Steven asked.

"Yes," she says. "I and a group of like-minded people decided to erect this barrier many years ago. I got elected the current caretaker, so it's my job to make sure it stays up and is monitored. This is how I keep an eye on it. When you two tranced in the clearing yesterday, I received a kind of alert, and I came up here and checked you out. Watch, I can zoom in."

She moved her hands into the dome and the view changed to the area she was pointing at. They had a bird's-eye view of the clearing they had been in earlier that morning.

"That's how you saw my blindfold," Roy said.

"Why do you use a blindfold?" she asked.

"That's how my father did it," Roy said. "I picked it up. Now I'm used to it. It helps me concentrate."

She reached into a pocket in her dress, and removed a small flat rock. "This is what I use," she said. "It's like a worry stone. I hold it between my thumb and finger, like this," she demonstrated. Then she placed it back in her pocket. "I suppose we all just use what works for us individually."

As Steven continued gazing at the small representation of the land under the dome, he thought about what he would use when he conducted his first trance. *Probably a blindfold, like Roy,* he thought.

"Traditions are good to maintain," Eliza said. "My mother used this rock."

Steven wished he knew if she really could read his thoughts or if her timing was just impeccable.

Eliza walked over to the sitting area and plopped into the chair. Roy walked over and joined her, sitting on the couch. Steven was enraptured with the dome.

"What do you think is your next step?" Eliza asked Roy.

"The only option I can see," Roy replied, "is to locate the grave and try to determine what's there – without digging, of course."

"Thank you," she said.

"Do you think a trance over it will reveal its contents?" Steven asked, still looking at the barrier dome.

"It's worked before," Roy replied. "I don't see why not. You've got your doohickey; we follow it and search from that spot. Jurgen said we'd know it when we found it."

"If he said that," Eliza added, "then it must be powerful, whatever it is."

"I'm sure I can find it," Roy said, "What worries me is I won't know what's in the grave. I've never been able to do that."

"Would you like me to come with you?" Eliza said.

Steven and Roy both looked at her.

"You can detect what it is?" Steven asked, walking over from the work table to join them.

"It's one of my specialties," she answered. "Detecting things underground is one of the reasons I live here, one of the reasons I am part of the group that maintains this barrier."

Steven smiled. Not only was she a wonderful host, she was also going to be an asset as they tried to solve Pete and Sarah's problem. Things were looking up.

◊

Steven led them through the low brush that was common in forests. They were a mile off the road they parked at, some thirty miles north of Clearlake. Roy and Eliza followed behind, easily keeping pace with him. Eliza was carrying a backpack that held water and food. Roy had required them to drink protection before they left the car. They were prepared in case anything went wrong.

"It's less than thirty yards from here," Steven said back to his two followers. Within a few steps the forest opened to a small clearing, enough to let direct sunlight filter down to the ground. There were two large fallen trees, and Steven rested against the branch of one.

"It's over there, fifty feet," he said, motioning to an open spot not far away. Roy and Eliza stopped and Eliza passed a bottle of water around. They all drank.

"Everyone doing OK?" she asked.

"Fine," they replied in unison.

Steven walked over to the exact spot. "This is it," Steven said. "At least, according to this thing. Do you want to try here, Roy?"

Roy walked over to where Steven stood. He closed his eyes and concentrated for a minute. "I get nothing."

"Let's spiral out from here, you following me," Steven said.

"No," Roy said, "I don't mean there's nothing there. I can't tell. I get a blank. Never felt that before."

"It's the barrier," said Eliza, stepping over to them. "Mind if I try?"

"Not at all," Roy said, letting her take over.

She closed her eyes, and Steven noticed she had her hand in her pocket. *Holding her mother's stone*, he thought.

After a couple of minutes she opened her eyes. "About forty arrowheads in the first twelve inches, all over this area," she said, waving her arms. "Hundreds of shell casing, too many to count. Lots of blood from men, women and children. Bodies there," she pointed, "there, there, and there."

"I'm not going to be able to determine more about the bodies," Roy said. "Can you see which one is the strongest? Which is the one Jurgen is interested in?"

"Sure," she said, and walked over to one of the places she pointed to. She closed her eyes again, and remained frozen for a moment. Then she opened her eyes, and walked to another of the locations. She repeated the process a couple of times. Finally she walked to the last spot.

She closed her eyes, then immediately opened them. "Oh," she said, looking at Steven and Roy, "this is it."

Steven and Roy walked over to her. Roy closed his eyes and concentrated. "Very faint for me," Roy said. "but I can feel it. I don't know if I'd have found it on my own. Jurgen is a fool to have sent us to look for it."

"It's the barrier," Eliza said. "It's very powerful. I'm going to remove it over just this spot, for just a few seconds. Go into your trance, and be ready when I do it."

Roy turned to Steven. "Do you want to join me?"

"Yes!" Steven said, and stood next to Roy. They closed their eyes.

Steven entered the flow, and within a few moments he saw the trance develop around Roy's body. He entered the opening Roy gave him, and together they waited for Eliza to remove the barrier under them.

At first he could only see ground. Slowly it cleared until they saw a corpse about seven feet under where they were standing. Steven could see that it had a sick glow, greenish, pulsing. The more he looked at it, the more sour his stomach became. He felt as if he might throw up, and he exited the flow.

Standing next to Roy, he recovered himself. Out of the flow he rapidly felt better. Roy ended his trance and Eliza opened her eyes.

"What was that feeling?" Steven asked. "I'm sorry I left, but I felt like I was going to puke."

"That's some bad juju right there," Eliza said. "A hundred times worse than any of the other bodies I've seen."

"The glow you saw around him," Roy said to Steven, "was the power his body still has. It's why Jurgen wants him. This was an evil man when he was alive."

"Could you tell who it was?" Steven asked Eliza.

"His name was Samuel Stone," she said, "and he's responsible for a lot of the blood in the earth here."

"Ever heard of him?" Roy said.

"No," Eliza said, "but his last name rings a bell. I don't like being near this guy. On the way back I'll tell you what I know."

Steven used the GPS to mark the exact location of the grave, in case they needed to return. He made sure it wasn't marked in any other manner by their visit. Then the three turned and walked back to the car, relying on Steven for directions.

◊

"So he wants us to mark the grave of an evil man," Steven said, driving Roy and Eliza back to Eliza's house in Clearlake.

"It's worth a lot more than a normal corpse," Roy said. "In his mind, recovering that body will make him enough profit to compensate for the loss of the tunnel."

"I'd say that man was evil enough," Eliza said. "His corpse would be as valuable to people like Jurgen as thousands of normal corpses. It's like finding gold to people like him."

"So," Steven said, "we were to pour that marker on the grave, and something that would have been able to cross the barrier would have come in and dug it up."

"Wouldn't have worked," Eliza said. "It might cross the barrier, but the bones would have slipped down as they dug. It never would have reached it to cart it off."

"Unless," Roy said, "Jurgen had come up with a way to counter the barrier in just that one spot."

Eliza scoffed.

"Don't underestimate him," Roy said. "He's resourceful. He stole that tunnel, he repurposed harvesters. He might have found a creature that isn't barred by your barrier and can counter the effects when they dig."

"It's obvious he knows about Samuel Stone, and thought we could locate the grave," Steven added.

"But he didn't know you wouldn't be able to detect it," she said.

"Unless he figured we'd be resourceful enough to overcome that," Roy said, "by running into someone like you."

"Now you're making me nervous," Eliza said. Steven watched her in his rear view mirror. She seemed to be thinking it over. *She thinks she might have been used,* Steven thought.

"If," she said, "this was his plan, you two didn't know you'd need me. I volunteered. But I do hate the idea of helping that little squirrel in any manner."

They rode in silence for a moment.

"What can you tell us about Samuel Stone?" Steven asked Eliza.

"I don't know anything about him exactly," Eliza replied, "but it's his last name. 'Stone' is well known in these parts. A character named Stone brutally enslaved the local indigenous people in 1850. He and his partner built a ranch not far from Clearlake, raising cattle. Made the Indians work for nothing, starved them, beat them. Killed them if they complained. He would rape their little girls, and if the Indian parents protested, he'd have them hung from a tree. It was so brutal eventually the Indians rose up and fought back. They killed him and his partner, a guy named Kelsey."

"That's horrific," Steven said.

"Oh, it gets worse," Eliza continued. "The Calvary decides the Indians have to be taught a lesson for rising up against their enslavers. While most of the young men are off hunting, the Calvary comes in and massacres old men, women, and children in retaliation for the deaths of Stone and Kelsey. Kills more than a hundred of them. The place is still called 'Bloody Island' to this day. There's a historical marker to prove it."

"Jesus Christ," Steven said. "Never heard about that in history class."

"A lot of brutal things happened here," Eliza said, "that people don't talk about. The governor at one point ordered the extermination of all Indians. They paid five dollars for every scalp. Some men brought in hundreds of them. There were many, many massacre sites. There's a lot of bad juju here."

"Do you think Sam Stone was involved?" Roy asked.

"Well," she replied, "I don't know. But the name Stone does make you wonder. Might be worth some research. If he was related to the ranch owner, or had a hand in the massacres, he needs to stay in the fucking ground."

Seventeen

Steven and Roy dropped Eliza off at her house, then continued on to the local historical society. Eliza had suggested they check there for any information on Samuel Stone and, oddly, had asked them to bring her back a postcard from the gift shop. It was only half a mile from Eliza's home, in an older section of town next to the city offices. As they walked from the car to the old building with the sign "Clearlake Museum," Steven wondered if the shuttered businesses nearby would be filled if not for Walmart at the other end of town.

Inside, they saw a collection box asking for donations for admittance. Steven dutifully dropped a couple of dollars into the box and they entered the main room.

It was one big room painted off white. It looked like every small town's version of a museum. It was quiet; it appeared they were the only ones there. Displays lined panel dividers, stationed around the room to give browsers something to walk past. A glass case contained some artifacts, mostly arrowheads and baskets. There was a small gift shop in an adjacent room next to the restroom doors. Most of the displays were about the gold rush, and they managed to walk past the majority of them in less than five minutes. As they approached the end of the displays a small older woman appeared and asked them if they needed any help. Her hair was pulled back in a bun and she wore a grey flannel print dress.

"Actually," Roy said to her, "we do need some help. We're looking for information on someone who used to live here in the 1850s. His name was Samuel Stone."

Her eyes pinched a little at the name, but she bounced back immediately.

"I don't recognize it, but if you'd like, I can look it up," she said.

"Would you please?" Roy said, smiling.

She nodded and left them, saying she'd be right back. They continued browsing the panel displays.

"I've seen nothing about massacres," Steven whispered to Roy.

"Me either," Roy whispered back.

They sat on a bench that was against a wall next to the exit and a water fountain. Steven noticed the gift shop alcove again. "I'm going to get that postcard," he said to Roy. Roy waved him on.

He stepped into the tiny room that housed the museum's gift shop. It was crowded with postcards, books, paintings, and toys. At the end of the room about ten feet away, a woman sat on a chair behind a cash register. She was reading a book. She looked up at Steven, and smiled. She was Native American.

Steven smiled back, and returned to browsing. As he picked a postcard, he heard the old woman return to Roy. They were right outside the gift shop, and he could hear every word.

"Samuel Stone was a brother to Charles Stone," the woman told Roy, "who had a ranch near here in 1850. Charles died at the ranch, and his gravesite is there if you'd like to visit it. He and his partner settled this area."

"Any idea where Samuel is buried?" Roy asked.

Steven walked his postcards up to the counter. The woman put down her book and began to ring him up.

"No, you'd have to check with the county office on that," the old woman replied to Roy.

"Do you know if he was involved in the retaliation against the Indians for the death of his brother?" Roy asked.

"No, I wouldn't know anything about that. We don't have anything about a retaliation."

The Native American woman behind the counter looked up at Steven as she handed him a receipt for his postcards. As he took the receipt, she whispered to him, "If you're looking for what really happened around here, you won't get it from white people."

He looked at her. "Do you know where I might get it? We need the truth," he said.

She took the receipt back out of his hand, and wrote a number on it.

"Tell him Lynn said you're OK," she said, handing it back. "He won't talk to you if you don't."

Steven was about to ask her who "him" was when the old lady walked into the gift shop. Steven decided to retreat instead. "Thank you," he said to Lynn, and walked out of the room. He heard the old lady asking Lynn about the status of a map order.

He joined Roy at the bench. Roy rose and the two walked out of the museum. As they got in the car Roy said, "Well, that was a bust."

"Yes," Steven said, "since it was the whitewashed version of things. This," he said, showing Roy the receipt Lynn had given him, "might get us what we want to know."

◊

"Oh, that's Joe's number," Eliza said, handing the receipt back to Steven and grabbing something from the refrigerator in her kitchen. "He's one of us working on the barrier."

Steven stopped, flabbergasted. "If you knew he could help us figure out Samuel Stone, why didn't you tell us?"

"Honey," she said, walking up to Steven and placing a hand on his face, "he's Native. You don't invite yourself to Native American things. You need an invitation." She walked back to the kitchen counter, working on dinner.

"Which is why she sent us to that museum," Roy said to Steven.

"Doing things the right way makes a huge difference," she said, stirring something in a bowl. "So you met Lynn?"

"I did," Steven said. "Roy dealt with the old woman."

"Roberta," Eliza said. "Roberta Cummings. White as a sheet if you know what I mean. She's been in charge of that place for thirty years or more. Folks around here seem to value the tenure more than the accuracy. Have you called him yet?

"I guess I should," Steven said. "What do I say to him?"

"Ask him over for dinner!" Eliza said. "We're gonna have a ton of extra food. Tell him to bring Tommy."

Steven looked at Roy.

"Go ahead," Roy said.

"Sure you don't want to do it?" Steven asked.

"She gave you the number," Roy said. "You make the call."

Steven dialed the number and said he'd been referred by Lynn. The conversation continued, with Steven asking about Samuel Stone. The voice on the other end proposed they meet somewhere.

"Funny you should say that," Steven said into the phone, "because I'm here at Eliza's and she'd like to invite you over for dinner. And she says to bring Tommy."

The call concluded and Steven slipped his phone into his pocket.

"He's coming," Steven said. "Said he'd be about an hour."

"Perfect," Eliza said, pounding a ball of dough with her fist. "This should be just about ready then."

"Do you need any help?" Steven offered.

"No," she answered, "just stay here and keep me company. It's nice to have adults in the house to talk to."

◊

Tommy was the same age as Troy and they knew each other well. They could hardly sit still through dinner. After dinner, Troy and Tommy went outside to play.

The four adults gathered in Eliza's living room. Steven and Roy recounted the history of their adventure so far, ending with their visit to the museum earlier that afternoon.

Joe listened intently. He was a handsome man with a striking face and black hair. He was wearing a t-shirt and jeans, and cowboy boots. He looked to be in his late 40s, and the way his clothes hung on him you could tell he was physically fit. He also had a warmth that was genuine and inviting.

"What do you think of their story?" Eliza asked Joe.

"Well," Joe answered, addressing Roy, "I'm glad Lynn sent you to me," and then he turned to Eliza, "and I'm glad you sent them to Lynn. If it is true that Samuel Stone was the brother of Charles Stone, there's a very good chance he has blood on his hands."

"For all we know," Steven said, "he may have worked on that ranch."

"Or been involved in the retribution on Bloody Island," Roy said.

"Or not," Joe said.

"But it's a good guess, Joe," Eliza said. "That body was glowing off the charts. Whatever he did in his life, it was bad. That's why Jurgen wants it."

"Canyon Fire would know," Joe said. "And only Kicking Horse can call him. If we brought the body to him, he could tell us."

"Who is Canyon Fire?" Steven asked. "And Kicking Horse?"

"Kicking Horse," answered Joe, "is the medicine man for our tribe. He is powerful, and he can call Canyon Fire from the spirit world into ours. He is the only one who can do this."

"And Canyon Fire?" asked Roy.

"He's like a Nazi hunter," Eliza said, "but in spirit form."

"Canyon Fire seeks a repayment of wrongs," Joe said. "He knows the past, he knows who did what. When we find the bodies of those who wronged our people, Canyon Fire reclaims the bodies and their souls. They pay in the next life for what they did in this life. He makes sure they pay."

"What would Canyon Fire think of someone who wanted such a body for their own profit?" asked Roy. "To grind up and sell to others for money?"

"He would view them as an enemy," Joe said. "The power of those who gained it by murdering our people is to be returned to our people. This is what Canyon Fire does. He returns the power stolen from us. And He exacts revenge for their crimes. But he requires proof. He would not act if their guilt was not clear."

"What kind of being is Canyon Fire?" Steven asked. "You said he is a spirit?"

"He is a spirit created by the anguish of our people," Joe said. "Many years ago, a great Elder named Owl Feather held a dream lodge with those who were the most angered by what had been done to our ancestors. They channeled that anger and Canyon Fire was born. He was named because a canyon fire is inescapable. He will live until the crimes committed against us are avenged."

"How does he exact revenge?" Roy asked. "What does he do?"

"He has many tools at his disposal," Joe said. "But the most powerful is the Manitou, which he can task with retrieving the soul of the guilty. If they are dead, they can remove the power from the corpse. If they are living, they torment the soul until death, then they claim it."

"I wonder if Canyon Fire would be willing to work with us," Roy asked. "This might work out successfully for everyone involved."

"What are you thinking?" Eliza asked.

"First," Roy said, "you'd need to let us exhume Stone's body. We take it to Kicking Horse, and he can confirm with Canyon Fire if Stone committed the crimes we all believe he did. If so, we give the body to Canyon Fire, for retribution of his crimes."

"What happens with Jurgen?" Steven asked.

"We don't trust that he'll keep his end of the bargain," Roy said. "We'd love to get rid of him, shut him down if we could. This might do it."

"How?" asked Eliza.

"If Canyon Fire could inhabit – or command the Manitou to inhabit – another body, make it look like it has power, but stay dormant inside until Jurgen shows himself and his guilt, we could bury that body in place of Samuel Stone, and mark the grave."

Steven realized Roy's plan. "Jurgen's accomplices dig it up," said Steven, "take it back to Jurgen, who tries to sell it or grind it up, providing the proof to Canyon Fire of Jurgen's intentions."

"At that point," added Eliza, "he's guilty, and the Manitou can take him."

"All that Canyon Fire would need to do," Roy said, "is command the Manitou to inhabit the body and wait until someone tries to destroy it for profit. Canyon Fire will claim both Sam Stone and Jurgen."

"A lot of your plan must play out exactly as expected," Joe said, "for it to work. Things can go wrong."

"We can at least find out if Canyon Fire can confirm Sam Stone's history," Steven said. "And if he was evil, offer his body for retribution."

"But," Eliza said, "if Canyon Fire won't go along with your plan on the changeling corpse, you'll be left with nothing to offer Jurgen."

"Fine," Steven said, becoming excited and standing up. "Then we pour the marker on another grave and when Jurgen is pissed it isn't Sam, we tell him it was the best we could find. He sent us into a barrier, what does he expect? We'll be back to square one with him. He'll give us some other task until he's happy. That's worst case scenario."

No one spoke.

"This is an opportunity to take him down," Steven said emphatically, "a way to pay him back for his greed and the torment he's caused people at Pete and Sarah's place. And who knows how many others. A way to stand up to him instead of just giving him what he wants."

Still no one spoke. Everyone seemed to be thinking it over.

Steven sat down. "Well, I think you know how I feel about it," he said.

"Do you think Canyon Fire will listen to us?" Roy asked Joe.

"I know that if the body committed crimes against us," Joe said, "he will take it. That is a definite. But if he hears your story about the plans of Jurgen, he may agree to your proposal. I do not know."

"What do we do next?" Steven asked.

"I will take this to Kicking Horse," Joe said. "Stay here. I will call Eliza when I get an answer from him."

"It is urgent," Steven said. "Our friends are being tormented every night. And Jurgen probably suspects we've located the body and will wonder why we haven't marked it yet."

"I will tell Kicking Horse it is urgent and must be done soon," Joe said, standing up. "But he operates on his own timetable, so be patient. If he agrees to call Canyon Fire, you'll need to have two bodies ready – Samuel Stone, and the corpse you want the Manitou to reside in until Jurgen proves his intentions. You might as well get prepared for that."

Joe turned to leave and thanked Eliza for the dinner. He shook Steven and Roy's hands, then walked out the front door. As he got in his jeep he called for Tommy to join him. Troy and Tommy ran over to Joe and Joe patted Troy on the head as Tommy climbed into the jeep. They drove off as dusk settled on the house.

"What do you think?" Steven asked Eliza, after they all sat back down in the living room. "Will it work?"

"Well," she replied. "Like Joe said, there's a lot of moving parts to get right. But it might. It would be *so awesome* if it did!" She smiled at him.

"Seeing Jurgen neutered would make my day," said Roy. "My year."

"Are you fine with lowering the barrier for this?" Steven asked Eliza. "Letting us dig up Sam and one of those other bodies out there?"

"I am," Eliza said, "because I've found the more power is returned to these people, the healthier this place gets."

Eighteen

Eliza poured Roy a cup of coffee from a thermos as Steven drove them all to the same location they had visited the morning before. Roy tried to drink the coffee from an open cup, watching for any bumps in the road that Steven might hit. He guffawed every time Steven hit one.

It was early. There was light in the sky, but the sun hadn't yet risen.

"Going to dig up bodies!" Roy said. "Just like old times!"

Steven smiled, remembering the steps they had to take back in Seattle to rid his house of ghosts. That had involved digging up a grave. It was not something he was looking forward to.

"We appreciate the use of your sheets," Stevens said to Eliza. "I expect you won't want them back."

"No!" she said. "What would I do with sheets that carried dead bodies? Creepy."

They parked. Steven and Roy retrieved the donated sheets, a pickaxe, and two shovels from the trunk of Steven's car. Then they all walked back into the forest, Steven again leading the way with his GPS. Wisps of fog hung in the trees. They moved faster this time, having a better idea where they were headed.

Once they reached the clearing, Eliza took two pieces of wood. She marked the grave of Samuel Stone and one of the other graves that registered no power. Then Roy and Steven started to dig. As they did, Eliza closed her eyes and shut down the barrier in the immediate area.

They dug for a while. It was still cold, and fog escaped from their lungs as their breathing got heavier. The sun crested the trees as Steven saw the first bones in the dirt below his feet. "Found it," he said, jumping out of the hole. He opened up one of the sheets and carefully placed the bones on it. Then he continued digging in the hole more carefully to find the rest of the bones, delicately transferring each one up as it was exposed to him. After he could find no more bones in the hole, he scanned the skeleton on the sheet. It looked like he'd found most of the important ones – hands, feet, ribs, the long bones of the arms and legs, and the skull.

"Sorry to disturb you," he spoke to the skeleton, "but this is for a good cause. You will be taking down a very bad man."

About the time Steven was wrapping up the sheet containing the skeleton he'd unearthed, Roy announced that he'd uncovered a bone in the hole he was digging.

Eliza stepped over to the grave. "Let me check," she said, her arm extended out to Roy as a signal to wait. She closed her eyes, and after a moment, opened them again.

"Oh, that's him," she said. "Definitely."

Steven brought the other sheet over by Roy, and helped him move pieces of the body from the hole onto the sheet. *We'll need to not mix these bodies up,* Steven thought.

"Samuel is on the yellow sheet," Eliza said.

"How come every time I...?" Steven said, stammering.

"Coincidence," she replied.

Once Steven and Roy had placed all of the bones they could find on the sheet, all three of them stopped and looked at the body they had exhumed.

"Samuel Stone," Roy said. "You brought this on yourself, you bastard."

Steven began rolling up the sheet. "I've rolled these up so we can carry them back to the car without fear of bones falling out," he said, showing Roy the handhold to use on the sheets.

"I'll carry the shovels and pickaxe," Eliza said. "You two can handle the bodies?"

"Sure," Roy said, picking up the yellow sheet that contained the remains of Samuel Stone. "Let's hope I don't trip. I guess we leave the graves open?"

"For now," Eliza said. "If things work out, we'll be coming back to put John Doe into Samuel's grave. If not, we'll put him back in the grave he came out of. Either way, we'll fill these back in as soon as that's done."

They lugged the bodies and implements back to the car. It was a long haul, over a mile, and they stopped occasionally to drink some water and rest. Steven kept an eye on Roy to make sure he wasn't becoming weak or unbalanced. So far he seemed to have as much energy as either himself or Eliza.

When they reached the car, Steven arranged the bodies in the trunk and then placed the shovels and pickaxe on top.

As they drove back Eliza asked them if they wanted any more coffee.

"No," Steven said, "but I'd take some hand sanitizer if you have it."

"As a matter of fact, I do," Eliza said, rummaging through her purse. She passed a small bottle up to Steven who applied it to his hands. He passed it to Roy. "Want some?" he asked.

"What is it?" Roy asked.

"Hand sanitizer. You rub it on your hands, it kills bacteria."

"Nah," Roy replied, "I don't want to get my hands wet."

"It dries as you rub it in," Steven said. "Try some, you'll see."

Roy opened the cap to the bottle and squirted a small amount on his hands, then passed it back to Eliza. He sniffed it as he rubbed it in.

"Smells like alcohol," he said. "I'd rather drink my booze."

As the sanitizer dried up, Roy held his hands up for Steven to see.

"That's really something," he said. "So now my hands are clean?"

"Well, yeah," Steven said.

"Then yes, I'd like some coffee," Roy said to Eliza. She opened the thermos and poured him another cup. It was still hot.

◊

As they drove back into town, Steven received a call from Pete. He passed the phone to Roy, who took the call. Roy and Pete talked back and forth. It was maddening to hear only one half of the conversation. Roy seemed to be trying to calm Pete, but it didn't sound like it was working. Roy updated Pete on their progress. He didn't tell him everything about their plan, just that if things worked out he'd be ghost-free in a day or two. After a while he hung up.

Roy passed the phone back to Steven.

"Well?" Steven asked.

"What?" Roy said.

"How are they?" Steven asked.

"Oh, they're fine," Roy answered, "Fine."

"It didn't sound like they were fine," Steven said. "He sounded upset."

"Well," Roy said, "he did say things were worse."

"Worse like how?" Steven asked.

"It's nothing," Roy said. "Just Jurgen trying to push us along, that's all."

"What?!" Steven raised his voice. "Tell me!"

"He's making the walls bleed," Roy said. "Melodramatics."

"You're kidding me!" Eliza said from the back seat.

"The walls are bleeding?" Steven asked. "Just at night? Or all the time?"

"He didn't say," Roy said. "Doesn't matter, there's no guests there. Apparently it shook up Sarah though."

"I imagine it did!" Eliza said. "What a little creep he is!"

"We've got to speed this up," Steven said. "Is there any way to see if Joe's talked to Kicking Horse yet?" he asked Eliza.

"I wouldn't recommend that," Eliza replied. "Native time is Native time. It works at its own pace. And a white man asking them to speed up is exactly what makes it slow down."

"Is there anything we can do to help Pete and Sarah?" Steven asked. "Something we can do remotely to make it seem less worse?"

"Not that I know of, we're too far away," Eliza said. "Oh – wait. Where did you say this place was?"

"About forty miles east of Medford," Steven said.

"Is that near Ashland?" Eliza asked.

"Yes, Ashland is close," Steven replied.

"I have a friend who lives in Ashland. She might be able to do something. I'll call her when we get back."

"Thank you," Steven said. "Anything that can help, we need. Sarah is pregnant and it's been going on for many nights now. I'm worried about them."

"Oh, Claire will love that," Eliza said. "She'll want to throw her a shower."

"Claire?" Roy asked. "Your friend's name is Claire?"

"Yes," Eliza said. "You know her?"

"No," Roy replied. "That was my wife's name."

"Oh, what a coincidence," Eliza said. "How long has she been gone, Roy?"

"A few years now," he said.

"Oh," Eliza said. "Not long enough for me to be asking like that. I'm sorry."

"No," Roy said, "you're fine. There's times I miss her. With Steven around, not so much though."

Steven had never heard his father acknowledge this before. Their relationship was much better than it had been while he was growing up, but he always felt a gulf between them. Working together the last few months Steven felt that gulf had narrowed. But he had no idea Roy felt his presence was easing his loneliness, making it easier to deal with the loss of his mother. *I mean more to him than I realized,* he thought.

He expected Eliza to make a comment, but she didn't.

◊

"Good news," Eliza said, joining Steven and Roy in the kitchen after checking her messages. "That was Joe. He talked to Kicking Horse, and he agreed to call Canyon Fire. It'll happen tonight, at sundown."

"That's great," Roy said. "Do we participate?"

"Yes, it's a private ceremony, but we'll all go."

"Have you met Kicking Horse before?" Steven asked. "Or Canyon Fire?"

"I've met Kicking Horse," Eliza said. "He's a very kind man. For him to act so quickly tells me he thinks this is something Canyon Fire will have an interest in."

"How exactly does this go?" Roy asked. "Do we go out to them?"

"Yes," she said, rising to make some coffee. "There will be a group of Elders, all major supporters of the barrier. They'll stage a dream lodge, probably in the longhouse there on native land. Kicking Horse will run the show, he'll call in Canyon Fire. Just go with what happens. Answer any questions they ask you. There won't be any games, they won't try to trick you."

"Do we bring the bodies?" Steven asked.

"Yes," she said. "And we'll need to bring some gifts for the bundle."

"Bundle?" Steven asked.

"Yes," Eliza replied. "The bundle for Canyon Fire will be at the ceremony. We'll be expected to contribute to it. The standard offerings are sweetgrass and tobacco, but we'll want to take something more, this is a substantial request and a significant offering will be needed."

"I have to confess I'm completely out of my depth here," Steven said. "I have no idea what to offer that would be considered acceptable."

Eliza thought for a moment. "Don't worry," she said. "I have just the thing."

"After the offering," Steven asked, "will Canyon Fire take Samuel Stone, right then and there?"

"Possibly," Eliza replied. "If he agrees to your plan, we'll leave with the changeling ready to go, so we should plan on going straight out to the forest and burying it. Then you can mark it."

"Wow, that means this could all wrap up tonight," Steven said.

"And what will you do once you mark it?" she asked, sitting with them at the table while the coffee brewed. "Go back to Seattle?"

Steven looked at Roy. "What do you think?"

"I think we have to be sure the body was retrieved," Roy said. "We should stake out the clearing after we mark the grave, and see who – or what – shows up to dig it up. Then I would expect to hear from Pete and Sarah that the ghosts are no longer visible. In fact, I think we should ask Pete to monitor tonight, and to call us when they stop."

"You don't think it's going to stop, do you?" Steven asked.

"No," Roy said. "I don't trust Jurgen at all. So to hedge our bets we should leave for Seattle as soon as the body has been exhumed and taken. That way we'll be there to confront him when we learn he hasn't held up his end of the deal."

"That means we'll need to be packed and ready to go before we leave to see Joe and Kicking Horse," Steven said.

"Plenty of time to pack," Eliza said, pouring them both a cup of coffee. "I sure will miss you two, it's been fun having you."

"I can't thank you enough for the help you've given us," Roy said.

"Oh! Claire!" Eliza said, jumping up from the table to go to the phone. "Let me call her right now. Might only help for one night, but at least it's something."

Nineteen

Steve, Eliza, and Roy walked through the doors of the longhouse and into a large, open space. Timbers angled upward to support the roof, exposed on the inside. A large open area separated them from a group of Elders who were waiting quietly for them to arrive. Behind the Elders, on the back wall, was a giant medicine wheel drawn in reddish-brown clay.

Joe and another man walked to meet them at the entrance. Joe introduced each of them to Samuel Kicking Horse. Then Joe asked them to step back by the door, and Kicking Horse returned with an abalone shell and the wing of a dark bird. To Steven it looked like the wing of a vulture.

Smoke rose from the shell Kicking Horse held. Using the wing, be scooped the smoke and pushed it toward Roy's shoulders and chest. As the smoke passed over Roy's body, Kicking Horse used the wing to collect the smoke that fell, and he flicked the wing towards the open door. He continued this process around Roy front and back, even on the bottom of his shoes. When he was finished with Roy, he performed the same steps on Eliza and Steven. Then Joe asked them all to join the Elders at the other end of the longhouse.

As they walked towards the large medicine wheel, Steven noticed the smell of burning cedar. He couldn't see where it was coming from, as there was no open fire, but the smell was strong and pleasant.

The Elders were seated on the floor in a semi-circle. Three pieces of wood formed a tripod in front of them, and a bundle wrapped in a blanket was suspended from the tripod by a leather strap. Joe motioned for them to sit, and Roy, Eliza, and Steven all sat on the floor opposite the Elders, where Joe returned to sit. Kicking Horse asked them to introduce themselves.

Eliza seemed to know everyone. In addition to Joe and Kicking Horse there were four older men. The Elders were kind, yet Steven felt a little intimidated by them. They all chatted briefly, exchanging names, hometowns, and some small talk. Kicking Horse interrupted the chatting to say that before they started, they all wanted to hear Steven and Roy's story.

Steven and Roy looked at each other, expecting the other one to start. Given the respect for elders that the room seemed to inspire, Steven waited for Roy to begin. Roy told the group the events they had witnessed over the past two weeks.

The Elders sat stone-faced during the story. If any parts of it surprised or amused them, they showed no sign of it. Roy concluded with his plan for turning Samuel Stone over to them, and asking that they infuse the bones of the other body to be returned to Jurgen.

When he finished, there was silence. Eventually one of the Elders spoke.

"You have had dealings with this Jurgen, before?" he said.

"Yes," Roy replied. "He tried to swindle me and a partner."

"Canyon Fire will not settle a personal vendetta, even if Jurgen is rotten belly," said another Elder.

"It's true that I dislike him," Roy said, "and have grievances against him. And he is shady and dishonest. But he is an evil man aside from that. It was his plan to steal Samuel Stone's body for profit. He stole blood from people without their knowledge for profit, including the blood of a pregnant woman. And he is terrorizing my friends every night as a way to force me to help him steal. These are the actions of an evil man."

More silence. Then Kicking Horse stood.

"We will start. Would you bring the bodies and place them here next to the bundle?"

Steven and Roy returned to the car and retrieved the sheets that contained the two bodies. They carefully walked them into the longhouse. Kicking Horse met them at the door, and Steven and Roy held the sheets as Kicking Horse repeated the process with the abalone shell, smoke, and vulture wing. Whereas he had smudged Steven and Roy once on their way in, Kicking Horse spent extra time on the bodies, going over them again and again until he seemed satisfied. Then he motioned for Steven and Roy to carry the bodies over to the Elders. They placed the bodies next to the suspended bundle.

"Please, sit," Kicking Horse said. Steven and Roy sat next to Eliza in the circle. Steven was worried that the conversation they'd had with the Elders hadn't exactly gone the way he'd expected. *Are they on our side in this?* he thought. *Do they see it the same way we do? Will they ask Canyon Fire for the same things we asked for?*

He looked at Eliza and they exchanged glances. She gave him an encouraging nod.

"Steven, Roy," Kicking Horse said, "have you ever participated in a Native ceremony?"

"No," Roy said.

"This is an unusual one," Kicking Horse said. "Canyon Fire was created by a dream lodge many years ago. He is a spirit that holds the anger and cries of vengeance for our people. The Elders here in the circle with you keep him alive today. They inherited the responsibility from their ancestors. Do not stand and don't speak while they work. They will open the bundle, and I will call forth Canyon Fire and they will speak on your behalf."

Steven watched as one of the Elders removed the bundle from the tripod and placed it on the ground. Slowly and methodically he unwrapped the outer layer, which looked like a red blanket. As he opened it, Joe inhaled tobacco through a pipe, and blew the smoke of the pipe onto the contents inside.

Inside was another layer, an interior bundle. Its wrapping was white, and looked like a very old material. As the Elder opened it, Joe blew more smoke on the contents, which was a yellow calico bundle. The Elder continued the unwrapping. The final layer was a black satin.

Steven was intrigued to see the contents of the bundle as the final layer was removed. There were five or six smaller bundles, about the size of a fist, wrapped in red cloth and leather strips. There were several leather pouches. Tobacco spilled from one. He saw a long braided material which looked like the sweetgrass Eliza had brought, and a small glass bottle that contained a clear liquid. There was a small gourd with feathers attached. Joe blew more smoke over the contents. One of the Elders rose and removed the gourd; it made a light rattling sound as he picked it up. Another Elder rose and removed a much larger item that had an animal tail connected to it, then returned to his seat.

"Do you have an offering for the bundle?" Kicking Horse asked. Eliza stood, walked over to Kicking Horse, and gave him the sweetgrass, tobacco, and a shirt that was old and faded. It had a delicate fringe, and a feather hanging from one arm. As she turned to walk back, Kicking Horse stopped her.

"Is this a ghost dance shirt?" he asked.

"It is," she answered, wiping a tear from her eye as she watched Kicking Horse inspect it.

Steven heard the seated Elders murmuring. Kicking Horse looked at Eliza and smiled. "You and I will talk about this another day," Kicking Horse said, placing it with the other items in the bundle.

Kicking Horse walked to the wall of the longhouse and turned off the lights. There were no windows in the longhouse, so no light of any kind appeared inside the room. Steven opened his eyes, adjusting them to the dark, but could not see anything. There were no ambient lights and nothing trickled in from under a door or through a crack. He held his hand in front of his face and couldn't see it.

A flame flickered as Kicking Horse lit the end of a two foot piece of braided sweetgrass. The flame was extinguished, and the burning end of the grass glowed bright red. Kicking Horse raised the braid over his head and swung it through the air, in a circle. The burning grass gave off a sweet smell, and the circular motion of the red ember was mesmerizing to Steven. The more he watched its movement the calmer he felt.

He became aware that the objects that had been removed from the bundle were now being shaken by the Elders who removed them. One created a light, gentle rattle, while the other sounded rough and heavy. A rhythm began to develop between the spinning red cherry of the sweetgrass and the shaking of the bundle rattles. Steven's mesmerization deepened.

Kicking Horse began chanting in a language he didn't understand. It lasted for several minutes. The intensity and loudness of the rattling increased, and the sound of the braided sweetgrass cutting through the air blended with the chanting and the rattles. There was a sense of something building, something being drawn. When Kicking Horse abruptly stopped, everything went silent, and Steven could feel a momentum all around him. All of his senses were alive in anticipation of what would happen next.

He felt a wind against the back of his neck. He turned, but there was nothing to see. He felt more wind, against his face and cheeks. The ground underneath him began to shake. He felt an overpowering need to stand and run out of the longhouse, certain that an earthquake was underway. Then he heard one of the Elders speaking. It also was a language he didn't understand. When he was finished another Elder spoke. This continued for several minutes. He continued to strain his eyes to see, but only blackness met them.

He placed his hands on the ground next to him, to feel the earth. It was rumbling under his fingers.

He knew something else was in the room with them and had been since the shaking began. He wanted to slip into the River, to see if he could discern what was happening, but he didn't know if this would be acceptable to his hosts. His curiosity won out, and he jumped in.

When he entered, he noticed Roy and Eliza were already there. He was late to the party.

Canyon Fire was already manifest as a burning wooden mask, floating in the center of the circle, hovering over the bundle. He could see nothing behind the mask. It did not cast light; its fire was not illuminating any of the people around the circle. He could hear one of the Elders speaking to it and then pausing for an answer, as though they were having a conversation. After a moment the Elder stopped talking. In another moment, the mask faded away and was gone. Then he noticed that one of the bodies was missing – the one wrapped in the yellow sheet.

He saw thin red wisps of fog swirl in and around the other body under the sheet. Everyone watched as the wisps moved in and out of the body, seeming to settle inside it. The ground continued to shake under Steven, and the smell of tobacco smoke was strong in his nostrils. Steven knew that Canyon Fire had accepted their proposal. The changeling was becoming a host to the Manitou.

He heard Kicking Horse chanting again, but from within the flow Steven understood what he was doing – he was summoning Canyon Fire to return to the world he came from. The rumbling under his hands slowly diminished. A long silence passed over the room, and Steven realized they were done, the ceremony was ending. It had lasted no more than ten minutes. Steven exited the flow, and sat in the dark for a moment longer until Kicking Horse turned the light back on.

The Elders stayed seated. One of them began to fold the items of the bundle into the black satin layer and wrap it up, incorporating the offerings they had brought. They watched as the bundle was slowly reassembled.

Steven was overwhelmed and he hoped no one would speak to him because he wasn't sure he could answer. Thankfully, Kicking Horse spoke to Roy.

"You may take the body. If he is judged to be good, the spirit inside will not attack. But if he is judged evil, when he attempts to open the bones the spirit will be released and he will be punished for his crimes."

Steven, Roy, and Eliza stood. Steven and Roy took hold of the ends of the sheet that contained the body. Steven wasn't sure why he did it, but he grabbed the empty yellow sheet and placed it on top of the bundle they were about to carry from the room.

As they lifted the body, the voice of one of the Elders stopped them. "On behalf of the tribe, we thank you for returning Samuel Stone to us. He abused and killed many of us; men, women, and children. Now his power has been reclaimed by Canyon Fire for the tribe. It is an ugly thing, but it is justice. Good luck on your path."

"Thank you," Roy said, and they carried the body out of the longhouse. Steven opened the trunk of the car, and they placed the body inside.

"Do we go back in?" Steven asked.

"No," Eliza said. "It's done, they did their part. Now it's up to us to finish it."

"Do you want to come with us to bury it?" Steven asked.

"You are planning to hang out there and wait to see who takes it, right?" she asked.

"Indeed we are," answered Steven.

"Then absolutely I'm coming," she said. "Wouldn't miss it for the world!"

◊

As they drove the twenty miles into the forest to reinter the corpse, Steven asked Eliza questions about the ceremony he had witnessed.

"Oh yes," she said, "I jumped in the moment it started. Didn't you Roy?"

"Sure I did," Roy said.

"I guess I thought that would be rude," Steven said. "I only saw the ending."

"The Elders all expected us to be in the River," Eliza said. "The only reason we were allowed to see that, considering that we're white folk, was because of our gift. They knew we'd understand and respect it, and could witness it the same as they did. If not they wouldn't have let us in the door."

"So that ceremony hasn't been witnessed by many white people?" Steven asked.

"I think the only white people who've ever seen that ceremony," Eliza said, "are sitting in this car right now."

"Wow," Steven said. "I guess that's pretty amazing."

"Vengeance is a tricky thing," Roy said. "Those Elders have a delicate job. It can get away from you quickly and become a monster. I admire that they've been able to keep it controlled the way they have."

"Don't think there haven't been discussions in the tribe about it," Eliza said. "Not everyone knows about it, but even among those who do there are plenty who don't approve."

"I can see why," Steven said. "How do you know when you've balanced the scales, or gone too far?"

"Trust me," Eliza said, "there were so many massacres of Native Americans in California in the 19th century, Canyon Fire could go on for another hundred years and the scales wouldn't be balanced. They used to give the massacres names, but there were so many of them they stopped naming them."

Steven checked the time on the car's clock. It was approaching ten p.m. as he parked the car for the final time at the side of the road and they removed the body from the trunk. Eliza walked ahead with a flashlight and the shovels. Steven removed the GPS from his pocket occasionally to make sure they were on the right track.

Once they placed the bones into Samuel's former grave, they filled in both holes and smoothed the dirt.

"Do you have the vial Jurgen gave you?" Steven asked Roy.

"Yes," he said, removing it from his pocket.

"I suggest," Eliza said, "that as soon as you pour that, we make a mad dash for those fallen trees over there. We can hide behind them. There's no telling how quickly someone or something might show up to get the body."

Steven and Roy looked down at the grave under their feet. "We've essentially created a time bomb," Steven said.

"Yeah," Roy said. "Let's just hope it explodes at the right time."

Roy unscrewed the top of the vial and as Eliza held the flashlight he poured the contents onto the ground of the grave. Steven half expected the sound of acid eating through material, or smoke to rise from the spot where it landed, but nothing appeared and no unusual sounds occurred – just the sound and sight of liquid pouring on earth.

Then they smelled it. And ran.

◊

They had been waiting for almost an hour. Eliza was monitoring the barrier and Steven was watching the clearing for any sign of disturbance or movement. Roy was watching from within the flow. The moon was out, and it was easy to see the entire clearing from their hiding spot.

"What if it comes at the grave from where we're hiding and stumbles upon us?" Steven whispered.

"We'll know," Eliza and Roy whispered back in unison.

"I'm keeping an eye on the area behind us," Roy said. "I'll see it before it sees us."

They sat in silence for a while longer.

"Got something," Roy whispered. "Two o'clock."

As they watched, a large man emerged from the forest edge and started walking toward the grave. Steven guessed he must be seven feet tall. He was dragging a shovel and a duffel bag.

"Jump in," Roy said. "You'll want to see this."

Steven and Eliza both entered the flow. The man was following a creature that was floating above the ground about eighteen inches, shaped like a spider but with at least a dozen legs. The legs moved incredibly fast, creating a blur. Then they would pause, shift to a new direction, and blur again. It had several eyes on its forehead. It hovered to the gravesite and stopped, then lowered to the ground. They couldn't see it anymore from their angle behind the trees.

Don't rise up to try and see it, Roy thought for the others to hear. *I don't know how far it can see with those eyes. Stay down. Inside the flow, too.*

The man dug his shovel into the ground and began removing earth. It was easy going as the earth had been so recently moved. He didn't speak or make any sounds, he just kept turning shovelfuls of dirt.

If he's evil, Roy thought, *let's hope he doesn't break any bones with the shovel.*

They saw him lift bones out of the grave and place them into the duffel bag he had brought. After several minutes he had completed the job and began filling the grave back in.

Once he was done the spider creature hovered up into view, leading him back the way he came. They exited the flow and watched as the man disappeared into the woods.

"Ooo," Eliza said, "that spider is going on the banned list. Just as soon as they leave the barrier edge, I'm updating it."

"Come on," Steven said, "we've got to get back to the car."

They traced their steps back through the forest. At the car Steven loaded the shovels into the trunk and then drove them back to Eliza's house, where they loaded up their bags.

"Goodbye," Roy said. "I'm glad we met you. Thank you." He gave her a hug.

"Please tell Dixon hi for me," she said, moving to give Steven a hug as well.

"You were incredible," he said to her. She hugged him a little longer than he anticipated. "Tell me what you're really thinking," she spoke in his ear.

"Will you be able to tell what I'm thinking when I'm back in Seattle?" he asked as they ended the hug and separated.

"No, it's too far away," she said.

I expect I'll feel the same way, he thought.

She smiled at him as he got in the car next to Roy and they drove off into the night.

Twenty

It was still dark as they approached Medford.

"Should we check in with Pete?" Steven asked, his eyes tired from hours on the road.

"It's early, but he won't mind the call," Roy said. "The older you get the less you care about getting up early."

Steven pulled his phone out of his pocket and passed it to Roy.

"Pete?" Roy said into the phone. "Yes, Roy here. How's it going?"

They talked for a while, Roy asking about the state of things and receiving long replies that Steven couldn't hear.

"OK, we'll stop then," Roy said. "We're about an hour away. Yes. Bye."

Roy handed the phone back to Steven. "Let's pull off and see them. Sounds like things are interesting there."

"What do you mean?" Steven asked.

"Claire has had a bit of an impact," Roy replied.

"The ghosts are still visible?" Steven asked.

"Yes," Roy replied, "no change there."

Steven took the turn towards the manor and after another hour of travel they pulled up to the manor. There was a red Volkswagon bug in the parking lot next to them, the only other car. There was a large white daisy in the flower holder on the dash.

"Must be Claire's," Steven said to Roy as they walked in.

They found Pete, Sarah, and Claire in the dining room seated around the same table Steven and Roy had enjoyed breakfast at during their earlier visits. Both Pete and Sarah seemed glad to see them, rising to shake their hands and welcome them.

"This is Claire," Pete said, introducing her to Steven and Roy.

"You're Eliza's friend?" Steven asked.

"We've known each other for years," she said, smiling. She was short, about five feet six, and very thin. She was wearing a long summer dress with a floral print, and had sandals on her feet. Her hair was bright red and curly, and it bounced at the sides of her head as she moved.

"We've been up all night," Sarah said.

"Oh, I'm sorry to hear that," Steven said. "The ghosts are still keeping you up?"

"No," Sarah replied. "I and Claire have been meeting some of them. It's the strangest experience I've ever had."

They all sat at the table and passed around food and coffee.

"Meeting them?" Steven asked. "Like, conversing with them?"

"Yes, kind of like that," Sarah said. "Maybe you can explain it better, Claire."

"Well," Claire said, "when I got here last night, it was obvious there was no way I could stop the curse or the blood. But there are so many ghosts here, I figured I might as well try to learn a thing or two about the place. Sarah seemed interested in what I was doing, so she tagged along. Before we knew it, we spent the entire night talking with them."

"At first I was a little leery," Sarah said, "but after I saw how Claire interacted with them, I realized I didn't need to be afraid of every one of these ghosts. Some of them were quite nice. You just have to avoid the bad ones."

"That is the trick," Roy said.

"And I will admit," Sarah said, "that even though they're nice, it's still disarming. You can have a very nice conversation with them and then something horrible happens to them out of the blue. I'm not quite used to that. But it was fascinating."

"We met a woman in the back utility room," Claire said, "who was washing clothes by hand. We talked to her for a long time about the manor, who she worked for, her family, all of that. Fascinating history about the place, around 1910."

"She has a little girl who is four," Sarah said, "and a boy who is seven. Her friend runs a school that the children attend while she's here working. Her husband is a logger. Wants her to stop working, but she refuses to."

"Fascinating woman," Claire said, "very opinionated. She knew a lot about this place and the family that built it."

"The only problem was," Sarah said, "when she finished the clothes she was working on, she'd say, 'I just have to hang these, I'll be right back,' and she'd walk out the back door into the yard. But she didn't come back."

"I followed her out," Claire said. "Another worker from the manor rapes and kills her while she's out there. He drags her body into the forest."

"Which is just so horrifying to me," Sarah said. "But then she reappears in the utility room, washing clothes, like it didn't happen. You can start the conversation again with her, she even recognizes you from before. You begin to forget what happened to her, because she's right there, working away, talking with you. But she always stops at some point and takes the basket outside. Creepy."

"We met a couple of others, too," Claire said, "just as interesting."

"Was there any diminishment in the ghosts last night?" Steven asked. "Less of them? Or did they all become invisible at some point?"

"No," Claire said. "Not that I noticed. They faded as it got light outside, just before you arrived."

"They seemed at full intensity all night long," Sarah said. "But I have to admit, I enjoyed them last night for the first time. Thanks to Claire."

Claire smiled and sipped her coffee.

"Well," Roy said, "we've been driving all night long. Completed our task down in California, and we expect the man who has been cursing the place every night to stop. At least that's what he promised."

"You don't sound too sure," Pete said.

"To be honest with you," Roy said, "I'm not. He's a scoundrel and he may not hold up his end of the bargain."

"Who is it?" Claire asked. "Do I know him?"

"A fellow named Jurgen," Roy answered her, "from Seattle. Trades in illicit materials."

"I've heard of him," Claire said. "Only bad things though. I try not to deal with those kind."

"Good idea," Steven said, "Stay away if you can. He's a piece of work."

"What did he ask you to do?" Sarah asked.

"He wanted us to locate a grave," Steven said. "We did that, and now he should stop. We're going back to Seattle to confront him, to hold him to it."

"It's a long story," Roy said, "and we should get back on the road."

"All right," Sarah said. "But promise me when this is over you'll come back and spend a week relaxing. You can tell us the whole story then."

"It's a promise," Steven said. They said their goodbyes to everyone and made their way back out to the car. Claire and Sarah stayed inside, but Pete followed them out.

"Sarah's changing," Pete said. "Claire made these ghosts interesting to her. I won't say she's going to reopen the bed and breakfast, but she seems less upset about it all. You know she's been very angry with me, especially since I asked you to help, Roy."

"Sorry about that," Roy said. "It comes with the territory I'm afraid. Sometimes to solve something you wind up stirring things up."

"I know," Pete said, "and I'm glad you did it and it's almost over. But this might just work out for the best with Sarah. The way she was talking to me this morning before you arrived, her attitude about the place was improving. She seemed to reconnect with the things about this place that make it great. You heard her, she thinks it's interesting – that's a far cry from when you were here before; she absolutely hated the place. And of course she now fully believes in your ability, Roy. Your idea to send in Claire was brilliant."

"I gotta admit," Roy said, "that wasn't my idea. It was Eliza's. A woman in California who helped us out. She's Claire's friend, it was her idea to send her over when she heard what was happening here. You should send her a gift certificate or something."

"I will," Pete said, "you just send me her address, will you?"

"We gotta get going, Dad," Steven said. "We need to hit the road."

They shook hands with Pete again and got in their car. Pete waved as they left. Steven pulled the car onto the main road and headed for the Interstate.

They arrived in Seattle eight hours later.

◊

Roy handed Steven the jar and Steven downed two gulps of the clear fluid. He felt it go down his throat like fire. Roy followed him and capped the jar. They were parked outside Jurgen's warehouse.

"You ready for this?" Roy asked.

"Yes," Steven said. "I'm ready."

"And what are we going to watch for this time?" Roy asked.

"Don't let him get under my skin," said Steven.

"Because?" Roy asked.

"Because," Steven said, "that's what he wants, and I make bad judgments when I'm angry."

"That's right," Roy said. "He might be satisfied and ready to grind that body up, or he might have found us out and be pissed. You need to be ready for anything."

"OK," Steven said. "Let's do this."

"That said," Roy added, "I want you to act angry."

"What?" Steven asked.

"*Act* angry," Roy replied, "not *be* angry. I think we should go with the good cop bad cop approach. I want you to be the unpredictable son. I'll be the steady and reasonable old man. He already thinks that's how we operate, no reason to change his opinion. You stay cool on the inside so you'll make smart decisions. But on the outside, be a little crazy and pissed. I'll tell you to calm down and be reasonable, but don't listen to me."

"Why are we doing this?" Steven asked.

"Because his M.O. is to throw you off with insults. We saw last time that it works on you. I want to throw him off instead. Make him feel uncomfortable. Don't let on about the time bomb, but shake him up. If we wind up having to negotiate with him, I want him to agree to my demands just to get you out of his hair. Got that?"

"I'm not an actor," Steven said. "What if he realizes I'm making it up?"

"Don't make it up!" Roy said. "Use your anger to give the performance. Just don't let it cloud your judgment. Remember our goal here. We may have to make some quick decisions and if you can keep thinking straight we'll be fine. If you get flustered and angry I'll be left flying solo. Stay in control, but act upset."

"All right," Steven said, sighing. "I'll do my best."

"Buck up!" Roy said, slapping him on the knee. "This just might be fun."

As they walked through the worker area, Steven felt the protection surging through his body. *It must spread around as you move,* he thought. They reached the door to the office and Roy opened it.

"Ah, the moron family!" Jurgen said from behind his desk.

"We did what you asked," Steven said. "We saw your guy take the body. Now we want your end of the deal."

"What body?" Jurgen asked. "I don't see a body!"

"Don't fuck with us Jurgen," Steven said, "we saw him dig it up and take it, right after we marked it."

"Oh, that body," Jurgen said, laughing. "I remember now."

"You better remember, you little shit!" Steven said.

"And you better watch your tongue if you want what you came for," Jurgen replied.

"The job is finished," Roy said calmly. "We expect you to leave the manor alone, for good."

"Well, I think the terms of our deal changed when you brought that new cunt into the picture," Jurgen said. "That wasn't part of the arrangement. I'm not sure I owe you anything."

Steven wasn't sure who Jurgen was referring to. He didn't want to give away anything he didn't have to. "I don't know what you're talking about," Steven said.

"Yes, you do," Jurgen said. "She showed up last night and ran around the place, trying to soothe the other two. You don't know her? Red hair? Thin? Perfect ass for fucking?"

"You're a pig, you know that Jurgen?" Steven yelled. "She changes nothing. You still owe us."

"Where is the body now?" Roy asked. "I gather it's worth a lot."

"Indeed," Jurgen said. "Far too valuable to leave around here. It's in a container on the pier. Headed for Japan."

It's not here? Steven thought. *Our plan has failed!*

"You can at least tell us who it was," Roy said.

"An old forty-niner named Stone. Brutal man, committed atrocities that if he were alive today would have made him famous. But since he committed them in the wilds of California a hundred and fifty years ago, no one cares."

"You wanted his bones for ingredients?" Roy asked.

"Originally," Jurgen said. "Then I met a buyer from Japan. When he learned I was going to come into this treasure he wanted to see it. When it showed up here earlier today I let him examine it. What a beautiful aroma it had! Intoxicating! He was impressed, said it was very powerful. The corpse you marked was one of the worst human beings in the history of the country, can you believe that? My friend offered a lot of money to take it whole, so I sold it to him."

"How much?" Roy asked.

"Not that it's any of your business, but since you did help me deliver it to him, I don't mind telling you it was millions." It seemed to Steven that Jurgen was getting off on rubbing it in their faces.

"What a slimeball you are," Steven said. "You're a pathetic scavenger living off the bones of dead people. You're as low as them come. The bones of a man who did what he did aren't worth anything in my book. They're trash, they should be left in the ground to rot."

Jurgen grabbed an object from his desk and walked up to Steven. He stuck the object in front of his face. It looked to Steven like a small piece of brown chalk.

"This is why you do what you are told," Jurgen said, brandishing the object in Steven's face, "and I tell you what to do. You are the idiot. An imbecile. You're only good for being ordered around. Whereas I run circles around you. I tell you what to and you do it. My intellect towers over you. You and your father are errand boys, nothing more."

"What is that?" Roy asked calmly.

Jurgen marched the object over to Roy, held it for him to see. "That," he said, "is what you worked to get for me. What you and your brain dead child located. Like dogs sniffing out something buried in the woods."

"It looks like a bone," Roy said.

"It is, you stupid fuck," Jurgen said. "You did all that work for me, but I'm the one who's made the millions. I'll make a hundred thousand off this bone alone."

"I thought you said the body was on its way to Japan," Roy said. "Why do you have that?"

"A souvenir from the buyer," Jurgen said. "It fell off as we were transferring the bones, and he said I could keep it as a token of his appreciation. Looks like part of a finger, doesn't it? Isn't it beautiful? Even this tiny bone exudes tremendous power. I can feel it, can you?"

"It's shameful what you're doing," Roy said. "Those bones belong in the ground, not ground up. It's obscene."

"You won't make anything off it," Steven said. He knew he had to derail Jurgen soon, say something that would take him off guard. "You're going to give it to us for our time. In fact, we're not leaving here without it."

Jurgen turned to face Steven, and glared at him. "You're dreaming!"

"We're taking it," Steven said again. "If you're not going to stop tormenting the manor, we're going to take that bone. We found it, it's ours, we'll sell it ourselves." Steven felt he should do something to further upset Jurgen, so he began pacing in the room.

Jurgen walked back to his desk. He placed the finger in a mortar. "Tell you what," he said, grabbing a pestle, why don't I crush it up, and we'll split it three ways!"

"We don't want it," Roy said. "Don't crush it. It's bones from a human being, show some respect."

"Oh, don't worry," Jurgen said, "I'm not really going to share it with you. I just wanted junior here to get his hopes up. What do you say, junior?"

"I'm taking the whole thing," Steven said, pacing back and forth.

"Oh really? You're hilarious!" laughed Jurgen, waving the pestle at him.

"Jurgen, stop," Roy said. "Don't crush it. Let us rebury it. You know that's the right thing to do. Please."

"You do-gooders really get on my nerves," he said to Roy. Then he stopped. "Why do you want this finger so bad?"

Steven and Roy looked at each other, but didn't answer. *What's the right move here?* he thought. *Act guilty. Let him think he's on to something.*

Steven looked away from Roy like he was trying to hide something.

"Ah, so something's up," Jurgen said. "This visit isn't just to see if I'm going to let up on your friends. You were hoping to get a piece of the body back."

Wow! Go with it, Steven thought. He looked at Roy again, and Roy's expression seemed to say the same thing.

"We promised a friend in California we'd try to get her the body," Roy lied. "That's why we came here today. Obviously we're too late. But we could return that bone at least."

"What does your friend want with it?" Jurgen asked. "I'm guessing it's not money. Some do-good cause?"

"Well, yes," Roy said.

"She maintains the barrier," Steven said. "She said if we could return the bones intact to her, she could use it to bolster the barrier for years, keep dregs like you out permanently."

Jurgen slowly leaned his head back. "Oh," he said, raising the pestle, "wrong answer."

He brought the pestle down into the mortar full force, smiling as he twisted it into the stone. They all heard the bone break.

Jurgen knew something was wrong almost immediately. Red wisps of mist swirled up out of the mortar bowl and surrounded him. In a matter of seconds Jurgen's face aged fifty years. He fell to the ground, twisting in agony.

Steven and Roy stepped closer to the desk and looked over the edge. Jurgen's body was contracting violently, as though he was being punched and kicked. Grunts came out of his body as the air was forced out of his lungs.

Steven entered the flow and observed the scene. The red wisps of mist continued to move in and out of his body, like sharp wide needles darting in and out. Each time they came out, they were bigger, extracting part of Jurgen, and his body shook in reaction. Whatever ability Jurgen had was being stripped from him a stroke at a time. With each moment Jurgen looked more and more like a frail old man. The needles struck at him relentlessly, extracting every ability and power left in him. Soon Jurgen laid still, without enough energy to move in response to the stabs and withdrawals. Eventually the wisps faded and the room was silent. Steven looked for any sign of power in Jurgen's body and saw none. He exited the flow.

Roy walked behind the desk and helped Jurgen stand up. He walked him to the chair he had been sitting in when they first entered. He carefully sat him down in it.

Jurgen was old. His skin looked thin, like paper. You could see the blood vessels, red and pronounced in his hands, face, and neck. His hair had turned white, and his cheeks were hollow. The skin that used to be a jowl under his neck now hung wrinkled and empty, like the wattles of a rooster. He looked near death, defeated.

"Ah," he said in a thin voice that Steven and Roy had to strain to hear. "You double-crossed me. I should have known better."

"You brought it upon yourself," Roy said. "Had you been an honest man, it wouldn't have happened."

"What was it?" Jurgen asked weakly.

"Native American spirit," Steven said. "It claimed Samuel Stone's body yesterday. The body you had dug up was a changeling. When it learned what you intended to do with the bones, and your general personality disorder, it agreed to judge you if you damaged the corpse. All your power is gone now, Jurgen. You won't be able to torment my friends anymore."

"I'll kill you for this," Jurgen said. "You're both dead."

"At your age? With your power gone?" Steven said. "I don't think so. You'll be lucky to make it to bedtime without croaking."

"You've got a bigger problem than us," Roy said. "When your Japanese buyer uncrates that skeleton, it won't have any power at all. It was all just expended on you. He'll want his millions back."

Jurgen's head lowered in his chair. He whispered something neither of them could hear. Roy placed his head closer to Jurgen. "What?" he asked.

Jurgen whispered again.

Roy raised up. "He said, 'Kill me.'"

Steven looked at Roy, and Roy looked back. They knew they had won. They turned and walked out of Jurgen's office. Then they walked the long march between the workers to the front door of the warehouse. Steven wondered if Jurgen might somehow come after them, but then he thought of Jurgen in the chair behind his desk. He could barely walk. He was frail and likely close to death. He was no longer a threat to them. He would be leaving his office today, and his few remaining future days, in a wheelchair.

Twenty One

Steven grabbed two bottles of champagne, one of the real stuff and one with no alcohol, and walked out the back door of the kitchen and through the utility room. Here was where Claire and Sarah had communed with the washer woman. He walked through the same door that she walked through every night, carrying her basket of clothes on her way to meet her death. He stepped down onto the grass of the yard, and walked around the back of the manor.

The weather was cool but the sun was out and the day was pleasant. It was late afternoon and they had all just arrived. Sarah had asked Steven to retrieve more champagne from the refrigerator in the kitchen. He went around the back of the house to do it, enjoying the view.

He returned to the gazebo, where Roy, Pete, Eliza, Claire, and Sarah were waiting. They had invited Dixon, but he was sailing near Cabo and didn't feel like leaving. Steven sat the bottles down and Sarah thanked him. She uncorked one and began pouring refills.

They had already toasted to their success and to Steven and Roy for their work. Steven and Roy had thanked them profusely and thanked Eliza especially for her help. Eliza and Sarah had toasted Claire as well. Finally Pete had stood and given a long and unnecessary speech about his and Roy's history, the good old days, and why he knew Roy was the man for the job. When he sat down everyone applauded, as much for the end of the speech as the sentiment.

There were a number of snacks Sarah had prepared for their reunion, arranged on small tables around their central table in the gazebo. They grazed from them occasionally and poured refills of champagne liberally. They were all staying the night at the manor, and none of them had to drive anywhere.

They had asked for a retelling of the final encounter with Jurgen, and Roy had delivered it with drama and flair. Steven felt he had embellished only a few aspects and he felt no need to correct him.

"So he aged rapidly?" Eliza asked. "To presumably his real age?"

"I was surprised at that," Roy said. "In removing his powers, whatever he had done to stop or to mask his age was removed as well. I had no idea he was really much older."

"I suppose he could have died," Claire said. "I wonder what it feels like to have your powers sucked out of you like that."

"I'm sure it's unpleasant," Roy said. "Perhaps it would feel like part of you has been cut out."

Both Eliza and Steven nodded their heads at this, and Pete and Sarah watched them, unable to relate to the idea.

"Would it wind up making you normal, like us?" Sarah asked, glancing at Pete.

"I guess it would," Claire said, "which isn't a bad thing. Except for the feeling of loss, that you lost something you used to be able to do."

"It would be worse than that for me," Eliza said. "It's a huge part of me and what I do. I'd be lost without it."

"I imagine then that Jurgen is lost," Sarah said.

"He is broken, that is for sure," Roy said. "And retired."

"When word gets around what happened to him," Eliza said, "you'll both be famous in certain circles. And I expect there will be a quick decrease in grave robbing. No one will want to risk what happened to Jurgen."

"Oh, the sign!" Pete said, standing up and walking out of the gazebo. "I'll be right back!"

"He has something he wants to show you," Sarah said. "He's very proud of it. And I suppose I am too."

Pete disappeared into the basement door and returned with a sign in his arms. He turned it to face the group.

"It's the new sign for the entryway of the house," Pete said. "What do you think?"

The sign read *Mason Manor Bed and Breakfast.*

"I thought you were going to change it back to Snow Meadow?" Steven asked.

"Well," Sarah replied, "we decided to split the difference. After learning what I did from the former residents of the place – thanks to Claire – I came to realize that the history of this place is what makes it so interesting to visit. It had to stay Mason Manor."

"What about changing the reputation to overcome the bad publicity?" Steven asked.

"Well, funny you should ask," Sarah said. "Look at this article that ran in *The Oregonian* a couple of days ago."

Sarah produced a copy of the paper and they all passed it around. It had been written by the guest who had taken the pictures at the manor the first night that the ghosts had become visible. It made Mason Manor sound like the most haunted place on earth. A couple of the pictures that accompanied the article showed ghostly images, and the journalist's retelling of the apparitions he'd seen were vivid and fun to read.

"Looks like he used a flash on those pictures," Eliza said. "You can't do that with ghosts."

"What an article," Steven said, worried it had hurt Pete and Sarah even more. "What are you going to do?"

"I'm going to celebrate," Sarah said, pouring herself another glass of the fake champagne, "because starting tomorrow we are fully booked for two months."

Eliza shouted a "hooray!" and began clapping. Everyone else joined in, raising their glasses.

"The author of *The Ghosts of Mason Manor* called us about writing an updated version. He's coming next week," Sarah said. "We'll be selling the book in a new gift shop we're going to construct next to the drawing room. And Pete is having plaques made to honor several of the ghosts we met. We'll place them on the walls in the rooms where they appeared, and people can read their stories."

"We're renaming the north wing the Dennington wing!" Pete said proudly. "What do you think of that?"

"I'm sure he'll be impressed," Roy replied.

"We wanted you all to enjoy the place before it reopened," Pete said. "We're the only ones here tonight, aside from the ghosts. Tomorrow will be another story. But you must stay as long as you like."

"It will be good to see this place running normally," Steven said.

"Thanks to you," Sarah said, "and Roy. I didn't believe it could happen. You gave us back not only our investment, but our home. We'll be eternally grateful to you. And you are welcome to come stay anytime. You have a lifetime invitation. And you should meet with the author of the book when he's here."

"Nah," Roy said, "you can leave us out of that. You should concentrate on how the ghost stories can help you reestablish your business. We don't want our names in his book."

"All right," Sarah said, "but you could become celebrities. I also got a call from a ghost explorer show. You could let them interview you. You'd be famous."

"God no," Roy said. "Absolutely not."

"How about you, Steven?" Sarah asked, refilling his glass. "Would you like to be famous?"

"I'm with my Dad on this one," Steven said. "He's the boss."

Steven glanced at Roy and Roy gave him a quick wink.

"And one more toast," Pete said. Steven stifled a groan. "Sarah has informed me," Pete continued, "that I will be a grandfather in about six months. Sarah, here's to you, to the stunning transformation you have made, and are about to make!"

Everyone raised their glass and cheered again. Steven realized Pete was the last to know.

The conversation and drinking ran on, and after a while Steven found himself wandering out of the gazebo and into the open meadow. The sun had set and the sky was beginning to darken. He glanced back at the gazebo. All the others were chatting between themselves, unaware that he had stepped away.

He laid down in the tall grass of the meadow, gazing up at the sky. The buzz from the champagne was running through him and he felt great. He saw the first stars of the evening appear in the sky. *Hard to see this in Seattle,* he thought, remembering his first night at the Manor when the night sky had been filled with millions of stars. *Maybe I'll just stay right here until they all reappear.* He closed his eyes and felt the coolness of the grass on his back.

"Steven! Steven!" someone was shouting from the gazebo. "Come here, you have to hear this!"

He opened his eyes and sat up. He stood and turned to the gazebo, which was now lit up by hundreds of tiny lights strung over the roof. It looked beautiful, almost as beautiful as the stars.

Although this is a work of fiction, the massacre at Bloody Island in 1850 is true. Over a hundred Native American women, children, and old men were slaughtered by the U.S. Calvary in retaliation for the uprising at the Kelsey ranch. At the ranch, partners Andrew Kelsey and Charles Stone kidnapped and enslaved Native Americans to work on their land and in their mines. They brutalized and killed many of their captives, and raped the Natives' children. Parents who resisted providing their children to Stone and Kelsey were hung from a tree at the ranch.

The town of Kelseyville, in Northern California, about 20 miles west of Clearlake, is named in his honor.

◊

"A war of extermination will continue to be waged between the two races until the Indian race becomes extinct."

– California Governor Peter H. Burnett
January 1851

Michael Richan lives in Seattle, Washington.

◊

The next book in *The River* series is

Ghosts of Our Fathers.

Visit

www.michaelrichan.com

for more information about the books in *The River* series.

◊

Did you enjoy this book?

The author would love to know your opinion of the book.
Please leave your review at Amazon.com, Goodreads.com, or your online retailer.
Your feedback is appreciated!

Made in the USA
Charleston, SC
23 September 2013